GOING DEEP

JAYNE RYLON

eBook ISBN: 978-1-941785-12-6
Print ISBN: 978-1-941785-15-7

Edited By Mackenzie Walton
Cover Art By Jayne Rylon
Interior Print Book Design By Jayne Rylon

OTHER BOOKS BY JAYNE RYLON

DIVEMASTERS
Going Down
Going Deep
Going Hard

MEN IN BLUE
Night is Darkest
Razor's Edge
Mistress's Master
Spread Your Wings
Wounded Hearts
Bound For You

POWERTOOLS
Kate's Crew
Morgan's Surprise
Kayla's Gift
Devon's Pair
Nailed to the Wall
Hammer it Home

HOTRODS
King Cobra
Mustang Sally
Super Nova
Rebel on the Run
Swinger Style
Barracuda's Heart

Touch of Amber
Long Time Coming

Compass Brothers
Northern Exposure
Southern Comfort
Eastern Ambitions
Western Ties

Compass Girls
Winter's Thaw
Hope Springs
Summer Fling
Falling Softly

Play Doctor
Dream Machine
Healing Touch

Standalones
4-Ever Theirs
Nice & Naughty
Where There's Smoke
Report For Booty

Racing For Love
Driven
Shifting Gears

Red Light
Through My Window
Star

Can't Buy Love
Free For All

<u>PARANORMALS</u>
Picture Perfect
Reborn
<u>PICK YOUR PLEASURES</u>
Pick Your Pleasure
Pick Your Pleasure 2

DEDICATION

To Jayne from Mr. Rylon, keep up the good work. (Also, don't leave your laptop open and unlocked!)

⌒ ONE ⌒

Sabine Reynolds bounced in her laboratory's ergonomic desk chair as she waited for the video chat to connect on her laptop's screen. It had been nearly a month since she'd spoken live with her mentor, Heinrich—better known as the illustrious Dr. Geld. Emails didn't really cut it, especially when he was being so uncharacteristically secretive in his messages lately.

Sure, the time difference was a bitch, especially with her wrapping up a project for the Monterey Bay Institute in California and him still teaching at the Fischer Center for Marine Research in Germany, where she'd recently graduated from the doctoral program he chaired. They usually found ways to touch base more often than they had lately, though.

Heinrich had been obsessed with his current studies, to an even greater extent than usual. He'd missed a few of their regularly scheduled chats and hadn't responded to her messages for days, even though he was the sort of guy who typically replied in an instant. Marta, Heinrich's wife, had laughed it off when he'd completely forgotten their thirty-seventh anniversary the week before. Only because it was the first time since they'd been married and she was a much kinder, more patient woman than Sabine.

An absentminded professor type?

That wasn't the Heinrich they knew and loved at all.

Sabine grudgingly admitted to herself that she was curious, and maybe a tiny bit jealous that he was having so damn much fun without her. The urgent yet furtive tone of the series of texts he'd sent her in the middle of the night—which had practically ordered her to take his call first thing this morning—made her wonder if he'd had a breakthrough.

It had been worth dragging her ass to the lab at the crack of dawn to find out a few more details. Besides, she couldn't wait to geek out with the man who'd literally taught her everything she knew about marine biology and chemistry. A minor finding wouldn't cause a scientist as experienced as Heinrich to go bonkers like this. He was in the midst of a major discovery. Sabine was sure of it.

After downing a gulp of her coffee, she checked her watch. Not yet six o'clock and she was already at her desk. Meanwhile, Heinrich would be finishing up his afternoon lecture.

When the incoming call icon appeared on her laptop, she clicked it faster than a mantis shrimp nails its prey.

"Good morning, Dr. Reynolds!" Heinrich beamed when he saw her. He leaned so far forward she could map every wrinkle around his eyes and mouth, a testament to a lifetime of laughter.

It still gave her a thrill to be called by her relatively new title. She'd earned that son of a bitch less than a year ago. The sound of it was glorious to her ears. The result of a hell of a lot of hard work. A compromise with the sides of herself that had warred between roaming the far reaches of the world and doing something meaningful with her life.

Staying in one place for six years had gone against her nature. If it hadn't been for Heinrich and Marta's encouragement, she never would have seen it through and reached her goal.

That was probably why Heinrich—who'd become a surrogate father to her—always greeted her in the same way, as proud of her accomplishments as if she was truly the daughter he and Marta had never had. Which was the only thing that could have convinced her not to respond with his title. Respect he'd earned. Still, it made him grin when she used his first name. It was the easiest way she knew to communicate that he'd come to mean more to her than a simple professor or colleague. "Same to you, Heinrich. Er…afternoon, I suppose."

That's when she noticed that the German precision with which Heinrich usually trimmed his beard and combed his hair had also slipped some. Tousled looked good on him. But weird.

"Careful…a few more missed haircuts, notes scribbled across your whiteboard, or goofy grins, and you're going to cross into mad scientist territory." She smiled at him, certain he knew she kidded out of love. It was amazing to see him so ecstatic.

"Now you sound like Marta." He waved away her thinly veiled concern.

"She's a smart woman."

"It's true." He nodded before barreling on, skipping their usual chitchat. His pen tapped against his desk furiously. "I have something important to ask."

"Anything."

He squeezed his eyes shut for a moment then blurted, "Come home? Work with me on this."

"What?" It shocked her to hear him refer to Germany as *home*, though she supposed it had become that because of him and Marta and the six years she'd spent under their roof after they'd taken her in.

Sabine considered herself a gypsy of sorts. She'd moved on more often than she'd stayed put in her life. Her parents had been in the military together. She'd traveled across the globe both with them and on her own after they'd been killed in a freak training mission gone wrong when she was seventeen.

Without clear direction, it had taken her a few years longer than the average student to decide what it was she wanted to do with her future, but when she'd met Dr. Heinrich Geld while he'd been on an expedition and she was working in a marina in the Solomon Islands, her fate had been sealed.

She tried to limit her relationships to superficial ones, given her history and her tendency to say goodbye often. With Heinrich, that had not been possible.

He and Marta had wormed their way into her heart despite her reflexive defenses.

"Sabine, please." This time he wasn't joking. "I *need* you. You'll get full credit. Co-researcher. I—"

"Hang on, Heinrich." She rubbed her temples, not quite awake enough yet to process what he was saying. "I'm not reluctant or worried about glory or some shit. It's that I don't even know what *this* is, really. You've been so cagey. Vague. Something with coral enzymes and their potential use in treating cancer."

"Shhhh." He motioned for her to keep her voice down.

"There's no one in the lab this early, don't worry," she promised, though his level of concern seemed like it was in the realm of tinfoil hats. Most people wouldn't understand their science-speak even if they tried. The rest would be bored to tears after thirty seconds.

"Okay, then." He spoke so quietly she had to rely on reading his lips to confirm she heard him correctly. "Yes. I believe we've isolated a substance that destroys cancer cells without attacking healthy systems. Or maybe it's reprogramming the rogue cells, resetting them to normal. I can't quite figure out why it's happening yet. I just know it is. I've never seen anything like this. Nothing even close. It could be...*revolutionary*."

Heinrich wasn't one for dramatics. If he was this worked up, it had to be promising. And concrete. Something beyond a theory decades away from practical application.

"Wow." She didn't quite know what to say. Or feel. Amazement, joy, and flattery didn't even scratch the surface. "Of course. If it's that monumental, I would love to be involved, do whatever I can to make this a reality. Shit, you know I'd be in regardless since you want me back that bad. All you had to do was ask."

Who wouldn't want to be part of changing the world so incredibly?

Renown or not, that didn't matter to her. Being present for someone important in her life, maybe repaying a fraction of what he'd given her...*that* mattered.

"Seriously?" He sagged in relief. "I'm afraid if I don't isolate what's happening, it could slip away. We need to protect these findings. They're powerful. In the wrong hands..."

Sabine couldn't imagine what he meant by that. Regardless, her mind was made up. "Sure. Don't worry, Heinrich. I'll be there. Can you give me the two weeks I have left on my grant here to wrap things up the right way?"

"Of course. I wouldn't expect any less of you." He winked. "After all, my partner should have the best reputation in the industry."

She gave a whoop as she considered things in those terms.

He clapped as she did a chair-bound version of a happy dance. Only then did she realize how stressed he had been lately. It wasn't exclusively excitement causing him to lose his grip on mundane things. The weight of his project was taking its toll. "With you onboard, we'll have this reaction understood, documented, and published in no time so that a cure can go into production as quickly as possible."

"Production?" Could he have already made a successful trial version? Be that far along?

No fucking wonder he was going nuts.

"Yes," Heinrich whispered conspiratorially as he came impossibly closer to his camera. It was sort of creepy and really funny because all she could see was his eyeball, giant-sized.

Which made it insanely easy to detect his biological response to the explosion that sent a shockwave through his laboratory, and her life.

BOOOOOOOOOOOOOOOOOOM!

His pupil dilated. He stopped blinking.

Heinrich's face covered almost the entire screen. In the far periphery, Sabine thought she saw a masked man pass through the frame. Or had it been a shadow? Smoke? Because flames were definitely flickering up the walls. In the background an alarm began shrieking louder than a howler monkey.

Shouts were followed by crashes. "We've got it all. Let's go!"

Were first responders on the scene already?

"Help! Someone help!" she bellowed because Heinrich couldn't.

And the whole time, he remained still.

Dead still.

"Heinrich!" Sabine didn't care who was listening in now. She had to rouse him. Black clouds had begun to billow across every inch not blocked by his permanently stunned expression. "Please. Get up. Heinrich, please."

Fortunately, the heat of encroaching flames melted his laptop, keeping her from witnessing any more gruesome fuel for the nightmares she would certainly have for the rest of her life.

"Heinrich! No!" she screamed.

He couldn't hear her.

Clutching her middle with one hand to try and hold herself together, Sabine dialed 911 with the other even though she knew it was too late. It took forever to explain to the operator that an emergency was occurring on the other side of the world. Silent tears poured down her cheeks as if she were right there in the cloud of acrid smoke with Heinrich's body.

He was gone.

Her mentor, her friend, her second father.

His discoveries—the priceless contributions he had been about to make to science and society as a whole—had gone up in flames with him.

Through silent tears, Sabine vowed to honor his memory in the best way she could. She resolved then and there to continue his work and ensure his legacy remained strong by any means necessary. And if this turned out to have been more than an accident, she would make sure those responsible paid dearly.

Miguel Torres bobbed on the surface of the ocean, twenty feet or so behind the *Divemaster*. Water churned beside him, looking like a patch of boiling water as first Tosin, then Archer emerged from the sea following their early morning SCUBA dive.

Turtle Town on the southwest side of Maui had lived up to its name. Dozens of the friendly reptiles were swimming below their flippers or slept nestled in the stone arches on the sea floor. A spotted eagle ray had even floated past, flapping lazily as it went about its business. The morning had started off right. They explored the pass-throughs and mapped out a dive plan for the guests they would escort through the Five Graves site in the coming weeks.

None of them hurried to exit the ocean. So he studied the palm trees lining the shore of one of

Hawaii's main islands not too far away. They grew on the hillside that rose upward to the summit of Haleakala, which pierced the clouds in the distance.

Even after six months of living the life, there were moments like this one when he still had to convince himself it was real. A gorgeous, nearly three-hundred-foot megayacht, which was a third his by some miracle, welcomed them home.

He'd finally found the happy medium between his wanderlust and feeling like a vagabond, destined to belong nowhere.

From the dive platform on their ship, Waverly smiled warmly at Archer. The love of a woman as strong, sexy, and wild in bed as her might be the only thing Miguel needed to make this scenario absolutely perfect.

The odds of finding a Waverly of his own on the *Divemaster* weren't the best. The boat was big, but not *that* big.

One thing hadn't changed. No matter how much they lingered, enjoying the sights and adventure of a place they visited, eventually they moved on. Leaving lovers and the possibility of building lasting relationships in their wake.

Miguel had indulged in a fling or two with their guests. They were fun while they lasted, which was never very long. He wasn't a greedy man, though. This was plenty to keep him satisfied.

Variety had its perks.

He sure as hell was never bored. Especially not when they had the clubroom onboard to pursue their darker pleasures in. Yeah, he truly was a lucky bastard. He must have been a goddamned saint in a past life to deserve this. Through Archer and Tosin, he'd found a lifelong friendship, a partnership, a home, and a family of sorts. Things he'd never dreamed possible.

So maybe he could get blessed by good fortune one more time.

"Hey, Miguel, are you listening to me?" Tosin asked, rapping on Miguel's tank with the hilt of his dive knife. The racket roused him from his thoughts.

"Ah, negative." He blinked behind his mask as he peered around. That's when he realized Banks, their business manager and so much more, had joined Archer's girlfriend. Together, they waited patiently for the trio of divemasters to swim over. Maybe Banks had details for them on the next group they would be hosting through the Divemaster Project.

Archer and Banks's brainchild, the program they ran from the megayacht gifted deserving people with a free trip of a lifetime. It was one of many ways they'd concocted to spend the billions Archer had inherited and bring some light to the rest of the world.

Miguel didn't pay too much attention to the scheduling, but he knew they'd been without guests for at least a week. Banks seemed to give them, and the rest of the crew, a break now and then. Honestly, he didn't really need time off to relax when his job guiding their special visitors was really more like fun than work.

Reluctantly, the three men removed their fins then climbed up the ladder. Miguel slipped off his mask and snorkel, dropped his regulator from his mouth, unsnapped his buoyancy control device, and swung his tank into one of the holders on the bench.

He peeled the top half of his wetsuit down to his waist then ran his fingers through his hair to try to tame it some as he joined the group.

Banks cleared his throat. "I wanted to speak with you boys to see if you'd consider accommodating an unusual request. I'd like to bring someone on for longer than the standard visit."

"Why?" Archer wasn't objecting, merely curious.

Miguel figured he'd let Banks do whatever he wanted. They trusted the guy. Owed him a hell of a lot. If he thought it was a good idea, they'd back him up. Make it happen.

"To conduct scientific research. Something too sensitive for the conservation arm of the Banks Foundation to handle. I'd feel better if we saw to it personally. It may also require us staying longer in the Hawaiian Islands than we'd originally planned. Perhaps for months instead of weeks, depending on how things go. Would that be okay?"

"I'm in no hurry to leave." Tosin sighed as he stared around, looking equally dazed as Miguel had been earlier. He hadn't always been so content. The stability of their new life had already made some big changes in Tosin. For the better. For the first time in the dozen years they'd known each other he seemed…secure. Looked over his shoulder less. Sometime soon, when they'd had the appropriate number of beers, Miguel thought he might ask what was up with that.

"We've got all the time in the world these days, don't we?" Miguel added.

Archer hummed, brushing his thumb over Waverly's knuckles. "As long as we're together, I don't care where we are."

"Besides, it could be cool to check out Maui too. Take a few excursions on land. Spend time with humans other than you knuckleheads." Miguel hoped they wouldn't decipher his code for…find someone to fuck for more than a one-nighter.

From the pointed looks his friends shot him, he figured they'd seen right through him.

Ah well. He shrugged, acting as if it wasn't a big deal. When Archer's father had died, leaving him more money than there was water in the ocean, Archer had started to question their purpose in life. Wondered if they could do something more significant than survive as nomadic beach bums who partied with lonely women on vacation by night, making even their kinkiest fantasies come true.

Miguel had laughed the idea off.

Until he'd seen what life was like for his friend with his soul mate. Maybe it hadn't been such a dumb question after all. Maybe his time here would give him a chance to do a test run at a real connection with a woman, something that went deeper than a night full of orgasms.

Banks cleared his throat. "Actually, Miguel, I was thinking maybe you could help our scientist out. She's going to need a divemaster and possibly an assistant when she's making her collection trips."

"Huh?" That would put a hell of a damper on his plans. He plopped onto the wooden bench seat nearby. "Why not Tosin?"

"Because I think you might have an acquaintance in common with Dr. Reynolds."

He tilted his head, suddenly uncomfortable with where this might be going. Especially since the scientist he'd have to babysit was a Dr. Reynolds, who was probably a gray-haired, spectacle-wearing scientist who would definitely disprove of his filthy missions. "Who do we both know?"

"Dr. Heinrich Geld."

"No kidding?" Miguel perked up at that. "I met him a long time ago. Before I knew Tosin and Archer even. He hired me as support for one of his expeditions."

"I heard." Banks's guarded smile put Miguel's senses on high alert.

"So this woman works for Heinrich?" he asked. "Any chance we could invite him instead? I'd love to catch up with him. I think you'd like him, too. You two kind of remind me of each other in some ways."

It'd be worth skipping out on his pussy hunt for that. He owed the guy a lot and would love to thank him for steering Miguel's life in the right direction.

"Not exactly." Banks sighed. "I'm sorry, Miguel. Dr. Geld was killed in an explosion at his laboratory last week."

"No!" Miguel stood in a rush, jabbing his fingers into his wet hair before gripping the back of his skull. The man had been a freaking genius, and far too young to be done making contributions to the world through his work.

"I'm sorry." Banks put his hand on Miguel's shoulder and squeezed. Waverly did one better and rushed to his side, hugging him despite his soaked suit and damp chest.

"Ah, man. That sucks," Tosin groaned as he and Archer shot Miguel sympathetic looks.

It took him a few minutes of staring at the waves to calm down. No one pressured him. They sat by his side as he got himself together.

"So this lady, she's picking up where he left off?" He'd help out however he could to ensure Heinrich's legacy was fulfilled.

Banks nodded. "Dr. Reynolds was his protégé. Highly respected in their field. I don't know much more than this... He'd somehow found a way to use coral to fight cancer. His notes, and everything related to the project, were destroyed in the blast and subsequent fire."

"Well, shouldn't Dr. Reynolds know what they were up to? She could redo the study, recreate the experiment, right?" Tosin wondered. "Why does she need to be on a boat for that? Not that I mind."

"It's not that easy apparently." Banks winced. "Dr. Reynolds was actually working on a grant in California. She has some correspondence with Dr. Geld and is piecing together what she can from the ruins of his lab. It doesn't sound like much is salvageable. And apparently he'd been very secretive. Careful. All she knows for sure is the locations he'd been out collecting from before he returned to Germany to study his samples. She may need to retrace his footsteps and start from scratch. The last place he'd gone before returning to Germany ahead of schedule was Hawaii. Specifically, Molokini. So she and Heinrich's wife, Marta, began scouring the area for any vessels that might be able to accommodate her for a while. Assist in her efforts."

"We should do this." Archer crossed his arms, spreading his legs as if prepared to battle for Dr. Reynolds. "I vote yes. Definitely"

Though the *Divemaster* had been part of his inheritance, he never acted like he was their boss, something Miguel appreciated beyond belief. As three dominant men, they'd learned to keep from pissing all over each other's territory to keep their friendship intact. Besides, it wasn't often they disagreed.

In this case they certainly didn't.

"Me too." Tosin nodded.

"Of course I'll help," Miguel responded when they turned to him.

"Good. You can start by picking her up from the airport." Banks grinned then shrugged. "I knew you'd do the right thing."

"Guess I'd better go get the helicopter ready." Waverly didn't bother to act put out when piloting was clearly her second favorite thing—next to fucking Archer—to do.

"I'm coming, too," Archer insisted.

The man might never recover from the time he'd let Waverly fly solo and nearly lost her. Good thing they'd upgraded their chopper to a six-seater. Plenty of room for everyone.

Banks handed Miguel a folder, not unlike the one he'd prepared with contracts the day Archer had invited Miguel and Tosin aboard for the adventure of a lifetime. When he flipped it open, the first thing he noticed was a picture of Dr. Reynolds, who looked *nothing* like he'd imagined.

Whoa.

Far more hippie than nerd. Sabine Reynolds was willowy, natural, and gorgeous.

Sexy as fuck.

Suddenly his assignment was looking up. "Let's go."

He snapped the folder closed and strode off to his quarters for real clothes. If he chose the black shirt that inspired women to stare at his chest and the cargo shorts that hugged his package, emphasizing his best assets, who could blame him?

⌒ THREE ⌒

Sabine spotted her suitcase on the revolving conveyor and marched over to intercept it. That's what she intended anyway. Her ambitious intentions manifested as more of a swamp-monstery stomp. Only her passion to carry out Heinrich's dream propelled her onward.

She'd flipped her internal clock upside down twice traveling from California to Germany then back through Amsterdam and L.A. to Hawaii. Spent two of the past five days in transit, and the three in between...well, they'd been horrific. Mental, emotional, and physical exhaustion plagued her after one of the worst weeks of her life.

It felt like losing her parents all over again.

More traumatic because she'd witnessed it. Slightly less awful because she'd been able to promise Marta and the rest of Heinrich's loved ones that he hadn't suffered.

Her zombified feet didn't keep up with her mind's directives, and she tripped.

Tucking and rolling to keep from smashing onto the luggage carousel and being dragged through those vinyl flaps separating the passenger terminal from God-knew-what airport underworld turned out to be unnecessary. Good thing, since her reaction time was disgraceful right then.

A strong arm came around her, steadying her. Then a deep voice with a sultry South American rumble asked, "That one with the rainbow stripes is yours?"

All she could do was nod dumbly.

Her savior steadied her then caught up to the bag with three long strides, hefting it from the infinite loop with one hand, even though it contained nearly all of her worldly belongings. *Damn.*

She might be tired, but she'd have to be cryogenically frozen like some of her samples not to obsess over guns like that or how they'd felt, however briefly, around her. Her hormones woke up and took notice.

Sabine subtly, she hoped, checked out the Good Samaritan as he returned with her suitcase in tow. The rest of him lived up to his sculpted biceps.

"Thanks." She offered him a smile, hoping it held at least a hint of pretty beneath the mountain of haggard. The black circles she'd spotted under her eyes in the airport's restroom a couple minutes ago or the gaunt jut of her cheekbones given her inability to eat while upset, made her doubt it.

When she attempted to take the bag from him, he held it out of her reach. "I've got this. Do you have any others?"

Sabine hesitated, unwilling to divulge too much to a stranger. An experienced traveler, she didn't waste a lot of brainpower worrying about the possible nefarious intentions of her fellow human beings. The good, helpful people far outweighed the rest. Still, she was no idiot. It paid for a woman alone to be cautious.

Too bad her entire being screamed that she should cave in to unwise temptations and let a handsome stranger take care of her precisely when she could use his broad shoulder to lean on and his big dick to ride before passing out for a day or two of solid sleep. Well, that middle part was speculation, an informed guess based on the bulge in his shorts. She assumed he wasn't storing extra socks or a taro root in there.

Apparently she'd stood still, staring and debating how to proceed, long enough to cross into the awkward zone.

"Oh, shit. Sorry." He laughed, showing off a great smile—super white against his tan skin—and killer eyes like the turquoise water she'd flown over minutes ago. "I'm Miguel Torres. Your ride, kind of. Banks sent me to pick you up and take you to the *Divemaster*. I'll also be helping you with your project as long as you need me."

Well, *hellllo,* Miguel. She could certainly use him.

Sabine hadn't yet decided if this was fate trying to make up for the pile of shit it had dumped on her or just another trap in a lovely package. A *spectacular* package more like it.

How the fuck was she supposed to concentrate with him hanging around? Miguel. Even his damn name sounded like pure sex when he said it in that sex-on-a-stick accent of his.

Sabine was no prude. She'd been called reckless by some, though she preferred to consider herself daring. Bold in every aspect of her life, she embraced her innate curiosity and was well-studied in animal behavior. Humans included. Sexuality intrigued her. She never hesitated to do some personal experimentation when the chance and chemistry presented itself. But if she'd ever needed to focus in her life, it was now.

Distractions weren't welcome.

Especially not the six-foot-something, ripped, take-charge gentleman variety.

"Are you ready?" he asked when she still didn't respond.

"Uh, yeah. Sorry." She shook her head to clear it, triumphant when she saw his gaze tracking the swoosh of her hair whipping around her upper arms. Misery loved company and all that. "Rough couple of days. I'm running on fumes."

"I can see that." He tugged the straps of her backpack from her shoulders before she could stop him. Somehow she got the feeling he would have scooped her right up along with it if they hadn't met half a second earlier. He was that kind of guy.

The type who took care of his own.

The type she'd never allowed herself to fall for, afraid that she might sacrifice some of her independence in exchange for his pleasure. The type who might consume her if she let him.

As though it had a single loaf of bread in it, he slung her backpack over one shoulder, grabbed her suitcase, and placed his free palm against her lower back, guiding her toward the automatic door. It opened onto tropical heat, which hit her like a shockwave and stole her breath.

Or was that the impact his touch had on her? Uh oh.

"Come on. It's not far to the runway shuttle. Waverly and Archer are waiting for us at the helipad." He matched his pace to hers though she was sure he could easily have had her trotting to keep up with his long, powerful legs.

"Archer Quartermane?" It shocked her that he'd come out to greet her personally. Surely he had better things to do with his time than fetch a lowly scientist from the airport. Hell, she hardly believed he'd agreed to have her onboard, despite rumors of his unimaginable generosity. Then again, Marta had used some personal contacts to get in touch with a man called Banks, who supposedly ran the entire foundation Archer had established, of which the Divemaster Project was only one small part.

"Uh, I guess. He doesn't go by that name anymore, though." Miguel paused for the first time. "We call him Archer Banks. Or just Archie if you prefer. He *loves* that."

Yeah, right. Sabine wouldn't be addressing the billionaire as anything informal until he gave her permission. Probably not even then. He was supplying a golden opportunity to bring Heinrich's life work to fruition. She wouldn't do anything to jeopardize it.

"Banks? Like his executive director?" She didn't find that as weird as others might. "He must really love the guy to have named his charitable foundation, and even himself, in the man's honor."

"Sometimes families are made of the people you choose, not the ones you're born with." Shadows clouded Miguel's striking eyes for the first time as he spoke words she couldn't have agreed with more. She was sorry he'd had experiences similar enough to her own to allow him to relate.

"I understand that." She blinked as she thought of Heinrich. And Marta. Poor Marta. Brokenhearted.

Sabine hoped that by completing the study, Marta's loss might seem more worthwhile in some twisted way. Right now a hollow sort of ache occupied

Sabine's gut. It hadn't been long enough for the authorities to finish their investigation into the circumstances behind the explosion. It could have been chemical. A deadly, accidental reaction.

Something completely innocent, though tragic.

Neither Sabine nor Marta believed Heinrich would have been careless like that despite his recent preoccupation. Though law enforcement hadn't found any evidence of outside involvement, she couldn't shake her recollections of those horrible moments. She'd been sure she heard someone shouting in the background. Thought she'd seen a masked man.

Which meant someone had stolen him from them. Intentionally wreaked havoc on their family unit. That realization only steeled her resolve to make sure the people responsible didn't get what they wanted—for Heinrich's results to disappear with him. She wanted revenge for the agony rotting her gut.

It must have also been written on her face as they climbed onto the waiting mini bus.

"I'm very sorry about Dr. Geld," Miguel murmured as he helped her sink into a seat and took the place next to her on the empty shuttle. Without hesitation, the driver headed off. Was this what it was like to be rich? It would be easy to get used to treatment like this, though she'd better not.

When she noticed the sincerity in Miguel's warm eyes, she saw something there that surprised her. Pain that echoed her own. "Thank you. Did you know Heinrich?"

"Not nearly as well as you." He held out his hand, palm up.

Sabine couldn't say what made her do it, but she accepted. Placing her fingers between his, she allowed him to swallow her up in his protective grasp. Simple contact could have a drastic effect on an organism.

Pheromones, pulse rate, adrenaline...natural chemistry could work wonders.

This was one of those times.

Grateful, she sagged, letting her head loll on the rest as relief replaced tension.

"Enough to know how inspiring he was. How decent and brilliant," Miguel continued softly. "When I was twelve or so, I bailed from the orphanage I'd spent a few years in. It was safer on the streets of Rio and better still away from the city. So I made my way along the coast to Búzios. I was trying to figure out a way to survive on my own, fishing and catching whatever I could for food. Stealing some, digging through garbage at resorts, and hiding out. Until I realized tourists would pay me decent money to show them my secret places—the best beaches and hidden treasures I'd found while exploring the area on my own. I would swim with them out to exceptional spots on the reefs for some quick cash and sometimes snag a meal while I was out there."

Sabine smiled a bit, imaging the enterprising kid he'd been once. No wonder he'd grown into such an impressive man. She respected self-made people. Those who forged their own paths.

"Anyway, Heinrich saw me hustling for customers in the town square one day. So he hired me, but not to guide him. He took me to a restaurant, ordered heaps of food for us to share, then asked me to tell him about things I'd seen. He had books with tons of pictures and had me point out different species I recognized. He wondered what spots I'd seen them at, how often, and during what parts of the year. At first, I thought he was a sucker for paying me just to talk. I was prepared to fight if he was trying to trick me into lowering my defenses so he could take advantage of me like some guys did."

Sabine subconsciously tightened her grip on his hand and he squeezed in return.

"Instead, he taught me things to make me better, safer, at what I was doing. He helped me identify new fish I'd seen on my dives and learn more about them. Figure out which were good to eat and the best ways to catch them. I never stumped him. Not once. He knew about every living creature. That goes for people, too. He understood lots about them." Miguel made it easy to imagine him as a lost boy when he stared into the distance. "He encouraged me to educate myself even if it wasn't formally in some fancy college. Told me about SCUBA and set me on the path to becoming a divemaster. If it wasn't for him, who knows where I'd be today?"

"You may have gotten there on your own," she offered.

"Doubt it. I wish I'd taken time to track him down and thank him properly. Hell, I didn't even get to say goodbye. The day his research vessel departed, I got held up by a tree that had fallen across the road into town. It took me and my four guests hours to hack it apart with a rusty machete so their van could make it through. Then it was nighttime and the return trip took hours longer than it would have with daylight. By the time I got back...he was gone. At least I'd given him my present, a *very* small token of my appreciation, the night before."

"Hang on, you're *that* Miguel?"

"He remembered me?"

"Of course. He often wondered what became of you." She thought of the stories Heinrich had told her about Miguel's mischievous antics, and decided not to mention his legendary ability to charm lady tourists even as a kid. There was one thing she figured she should divulge, however. Heinrich would have wanted her to pass this along. "You made him a necklace. Of sea glass and acai seeds tinted with vegetable dyes."

Miguel's gaze whipped to hers. "Yeah."

"He never took it off." Sabine's eyes welled for the thousandth time in the past few days. "I think he assumed something terrible had happened to you. Feared the worst. He was going to ask you to go with him, you know? To Germany. But he never got the chance. The next year, when they returned, you were gone."

She often thought that was why Heinrich had invited her to join his program after only knowing her a few weeks. If it hadn't been for Miguel's influence on him, who knew where she would be today either?

It was funny sometimes, the way the universe worked.

"Well, shit." Miguel looked away then, swallowing hard. "Yeah. After he left, I did, too. I'd saved enough that I was able to start taking classes and got certified. Then I moved around constantly, going where there was work and something new to discover. I didn't have a lot, certainly not internet or a computer or anything like that until recently. I wish I could have kept in touch."

Reluctantly Sabine shook free of his hold. She reached across him to grab her backpack. If she took longer than absolutely necessary while leaning over so she could soak in his strength and catalog the hard planes of his taut chest and abdomen in the process, who could blame her?

It didn't take much searching to find what she was looking for. She knew exactly where she'd put it, wrapped in a scarf for safekeeping.

Once she had it, she took the hand he'd recently offered her and unfurled his loose fist. Then she placed the necklace in his palm, marveling at how dainty it looked there. "Marta, Heinrich's wife, told me to take this for good luck. You should have it back."

He stared at it for a few moments, as if trying to decipher the meaning of it all. Then he shook his head, disheveling his thick, inky hair. "She's right. It sounds like you could use it. Besides, this will look prettier on you than me."

Miguel took the ends of the deceptively sturdy strands and wound them around her neck, slipping the shell on one side through the hoop of fibers on the other. His knuckles brushed along her collarbones as he admired his handiwork, which now decorated her skin.

She shivered.

"What I could really use is your help." She laid her hands on his forearms then, curling her fingers around them as far as she could reach, unwilling to let go now that she'd found an ally. If he'd impressed Heinrich at twelve, she had no doubt he would be a major asset to her research and collection efforts.

He rested his forehead on hers and whispered, "You've got it. We'll make this right. For Heinrich."

The tiny flash of the vulnerable child he'd been only endeared him to her more. Heinrich had liked to take in strays. Like her. Like him. Except he'd slipped through the cracks.

This time would be different, she promised herself. She murmured, "Thank you."

Sabine didn't question her instincts. She leaned forward and sealed their promise with a kiss.

FOUR

Miguel couldn't say women surprised him often. However, Sabine had already managed it more than once in the ten minutes he'd known her. Ferociously determined, yet sweet underneath, she appealed to him even more than the thought of diving in Palau, his favorite SCUBA destination.

So he dove into her instead, deepening the kiss she'd given him to seal their deal in the most delicious of ways. He'd barely had time to register the cinnamon flavor of the gum she'd obviously been chewing recently along with the expert press of her lush lips on his before the flicker of her tongue against his mouth urged him to shed his veneer of civility.

Unleashing his animal instincts, which seemed to be her thing if her encouraging moan was any indication, he slid his hand to the nape of her neck and wrapped his fingers around her. Miguel pinned her in place for better access as he accepted the invitation issued by her parted lips and plundered her mouth. He should stop before he scared her off.

He couldn't.

Miguel leaned in closer, pressing her against the seat. Her short, blunt nails dug into his forearms, begging for more, promising she could handle the full force of his desire.

"What's the hold up? Need help with her luggage?" Archer asked as he boarded the bus, which must have stopped some time ago, though Miguel and Sabine had been totally oblivious to their arrival. Waverly followed a step behind.

Sabine jerked away, attempting to disguise the true cause of their delay. Fuck that. She was his for the duration of her stay and it would be best if everyone knew it up front.

Sabine included.

After just a taste, he craved more. And he would have it. Have her.

Miguel stole one final sample of her spiciness before slowly backing off. He allowed a slow grin to spread across his face as he observed her dilated pupils and the color he'd tongue-fucked back into her cheeks. At least he'd been able to do that for her. She'd looked ready to drop when he spotted her in the terminal.

Instead of coddling her as he'd intended, he'd pushed her. Or had he accepted her challenge? Either way, once the thrill of their meeting wore off, she was going to crash. Hard.

Shit. They needed to get going.

"Seriously, dude?" Archer gave them a resounding slow clap for their sexy performance. "That might be a record, even for you."

Miguel shot his friend the finger, mostly because he didn't want Sabine to think their kiss had been anything like his previous seductions. It had been a hell of a long time. Okay, more like *never* since he'd found this kind of immediate connection with someone. Sexual attraction, sure, but also something...deeper. Rather than fuck it up before it got going, he'd like to see where it took them.

Hopefully their journey together began with his bed and ended up in the ship's clubroom.

Saving the day, Waverly greeted their resident scientist as if it was no big deal that she'd been sucking face with him a few moments earlier. "Welcome to paradise. The weather here is steamy, and the men are even hotter."

Sabine laughed and rose, finger-combing her hair as she made her way to the couple to introduce herself.

Thank. You. He owed Waverly big time.

From behind Sabine's back, he blew Waverly a kiss. She winked in return as Archer shook Sabine's hand and reassured her they'd support her mission in any way possible. Waverly didn't stop there. She went in for a full-on hug, offering her condolences. Now there was a sight Miguel could appreciate.

Two gorgeous women, one tall, sophisticated, and dark-haired, the other more of a free-loving earthy type with wavy natural golden hair, dove-gray eyes, and rocking curves. The necklace he'd made close to twenty years ago, tied in a place of honor around her delicate throat, made it seem like her coming here, now, might be some kind of sign or the answer to prayer he didn't realize he'd uttered.

If he believed in shit like that.

He snagged Sabine's backpack and suitcase, impressed that she could travel so light. Anxious to have her settled in, he wandered closer to the doorway. They took the hint, exiting the bus.

"Thanks," he said to the driver before passing over an insane tip. In addition to living on the *Divemaster* without any room or board expenses, Miguel, Tosin, and Archer each collected incredible salaries from the Divemaster Project for entertaining their guests and keeping them safe on their complimentary retreats.

Though they'd argued with Banks that getting paid any more than minimum wage to work a dream job was unnecessary, the guy had refused to give them a pay cut. Of course, Miguel could legally sell his third of the *Divemaster* at any time and become instantly rich as fuck. Why would he, though, when he had far more than he'd ever wanted already?

Less than a year ago, his entire life had become a dream come true.

Now all he needed was someone besides his best friends to share it with. Watching Archer with Waverly had shown him what it could be like to have a companion, a lover, an intimate and lasting relationship. He hated to admit he'd been jealous of one of his partners. Yet he had been.

It might not become a forever thing, but if she was down with it, he planned to dip his toe in the relationship pool for himself with Sabine while she was around. Why not try something different?

The bus driver tipped his hat and grinned. "Have fun. Don't bother behaving yourself."

"I never do, man." Miguel slapped the guy on the shoulder before disembarking.

By the time he'd crossed to the chopper—a serious upgrade from the one they'd had originally—everyone else had climbed inside. So he handed up the suitcase to Archer then joined Sabine in the back bench seat. U-shaped, the buttery leather couch could hold four adults easily. Waverly and Archer had captain-style chairs up front.

Though they'd never used it before, Miguel eyed the smoked glass partition that could be raised between the pilots and the passengers. Possibilities for another day.

He took the spot nearest the windows on the left side of the cabin and rested one arm along the back of the seat. Of course that meant he draped it over Sabine's shoulders, too. At odds with the confidence and competence she exuded even at what had to be a low point in her life, her petite frame fit perfectly in the crook of his elbow. He tucked her against his side so that she could see better out his window. If that meant they snuggled while she did, he'd take one for the team.

Together they admired the scenery as Waverly launched them into the air. They rose above the east coast of Maui. From their bird's eye view, the Hana Highway snaked between waves and cliffs. Occasionally they caught sight of a sandy beach in a range of colors— white, red, and black—nestled into hidden coves before veering off to the west in a drastic arc that tugged at Miguel's guts and made him want to whoop simultaneously.

He held Sabine to him, bracing her against the G-forces. Without so much as blinking, she kept her stare glued to the landscape below. He couldn't blame her.

The island fascinated him with its epic variety of ecosystems. Lush on this side, practically a desert by the time you got to Ka'annapali in the northwest, although it would only take an hour to drive that far. In between, mighty Haleakala rose over ten-thousand feet above sea level, stretching into the clouds.

"Do you think we can see the astrophysical complex from here?" Sabine asked, referring to the mass of ground-based telescopes on the peak of the volcano. Figured she'd geek out about that instead of most every other woman on the planet, who'd be satisfied with pretty colors in the sky during the legendary sunrises or sunsets seen from the peak.

"Nah, we're not high enough, sorry," Waverly called from the front.

"Ah, that's okay." Sabine shrugged and went back to peering around below them.

Would she be bored with Miguel? Though he knew a shit ton about diving and the underwater world, he'd never been accused of being a genius. He'd have to distract her with some of his other skills to make up for his lack of formal education.

With a wolfish grin on his face, he followed the direction of her gaze.

The emerald jungle of the Iao Valley lined the edge of his sight as they swung around the south side of the volcano's crater. If Sabine hadn't just traversed half the globe after losing someone so important to her, Miguel would have put in a request for Waverly to buzz some of the gorgeous waterfalls at its heart.

Below them, ash fields and scorched earth could have convinced him he'd stepped into Mordor. It was beautiful in its own way. Unusual, desolate, and stark. Beside him, Sabine nestled closer for a better view. He smiled and kissed her forehead before returning his attention to the awe-inspiring landscape.

Zipping over Wailea and its mansions, owned by some of the most famous people in the world, they soon approached the ocean on the southwest side of the island. Gorgeous water, in a million hues of blue and green, welcomed them home. No matter where she was anchored, the *Divemaster* would always be that for him. It was a monumental change from their previous nomadic lifestyle. It allowed them some permanence without tying them down.

It didn't take long to spot it.

"Wow. Is *that* your ship, Archer?" Sabine gasped. "It's beautiful. And huge. Absolutely nothing like the research vessels I've worked on before."

"No. It's the ship I own part of, along with Miguel and Tosin," he corrected. "She's where we live and work. Our sanctuary. You're welcome to call it the same for as long as you'd like."

Sabine yanked her stare from the megayacht for a moment to peer up at Miguel with questions in her gaze. They could discuss those later.

He shrugged then gestured with his chin at the ship, which grew larger in their view as they approached. She was a beautiful bitch, that was for certain. Gleaming in the sunlight, her triple teak decks, complete with a pool, called out to him, encouraging him to be lazy. Meanwhile, inside, luxuries abounded, from the wide-open lounges to the state of the art kitchen, and living quarters that would rival any of the estates they'd flown over moments ago.

From here you couldn't even see his absolute favorite part.

The dive center and platforms.

It was everything he could ever have dreamed of, if he'd been wildly outrageous with his fantasies. Truly, the *Divemaster* was so much more than he could have imagined. He didn't believe at first that real people— hell, that *he*—could really live like that.

Sometimes he still felt kind of guilty about it.

The charity work they were doing with the Divemaster Project and the even more unimaginable scope of the Banks Foundation as a whole helped to ease his conscience. What they used was only a drop in the bucket of billions Archer could have hoarded for himself, yet had chosen to share with his friends and the rest of the less fortunate people in the world.

Sabine's research was only one example of the good they were doing. So Miguel figured it was okay to enjoy a "little" something for themselves while they were at it.

He'd never claimed to be a saint.

Quite the opposite, actually.

Waverly lowered them toward the helipad as gracefully as a butterfly settling onto a delicate blossom. He had no idea how she managed to hit a moving target and make it seem so easy.

As they disembarked, Captain Alex was waiting to greet them. "It's a pleasure to have you onboard, Dr. Reynolds."

"Thank you. Though I do wish it was under different circumstances, I'm so grateful for your help. All of you." She sighed, wavering slightly as the gentle motion of the *Divemaster* rocked her. As Miguel had predicted, she was fading. Fast.

"Where's Banks?" Archer wondered.

It wasn't like him not to welcome guests personally, especially one as important as Sabine.

"He's overseeing the retrofit of the space where Dr. Reynolds's laboratory will go. There have been deliveries and installers messing up my decks the whole damn day." Captain Alex liked things tidy on his ship.

Sabine winced. "I'm sorry."

"Not your fault," Miguel reassured her before glaring at Captain Alex.

The man only smiled smugly before staring pointedly at the possessive hand Miguel had laid on Sabine's waist. Had the captain been fucking with Miguel?

Apparently his claim had not gone unnoticed. Perfect.

Captain Alex waved away Sabine's apology. "Don't worry, we'll have it cleaned up before the sun sets. I just like these kids to think I'm a grumpy old bastard sometimes. To keep them in line, you know. I will ask you to take your sneakers off, please. No footwear is allowed to be worn beyond the entries to the ship."

"Oh." Sabine gave what might have been a laugh if she wasn't wiped out. Instead, it sounded more like a huff. She toed off her shoes with a wan smile. "Never did like wearing them much anyway."

"Swimwear is optional as well. Feel free to lose as much of your clothing as you like," Miguel rasped in her ear.

Sabine's shoulders shook a bit. She hardly responded otherwise.

Miguel figured on a good day she'd have handed him his balls for such a brazen suggestion in front of company she intended to impress.

Captain Alex frowned when the extent of her condition became obvious. Then he said to Miguel, "Banks spoke to you about where Dr. Reynolds will be staying, correct? Would you like to show her to her room or should I call for one of the stewardesses?"

"I've got this." He nodded at the gathering, then led Sabine inside toward the glass elevator that ran through the heart of the ship. When he stepped inside it, he intentionally poked the button for his own floor, not hers.

FIVE

"Is this place for real?" Sabine whispered to herself.

Squinting to protect her eyes against the starbursts glinting off every polished surface surrounding them, she gawked as they descended through deck after deck. The décor and furnishings weren't the kind that made her think of museums or Baroque castles, thankfully.

Decadent, yes. Gaudy, no.

The boat's atmosphere felt warm and soothing. Relaxation washed over her, only adding to the weight in her bones. She hoped it wasn't a half-mile walk to her cabin. The thought of a bunk, however hard and narrow, nearly had her weeping.

She was surprised when they stopped on a level above the waterline. Real windows looked out onto the ocean from the lobby. Staff quarters usually consisted of tiny caves on the lowest deck of a ship. She'd consider herself lucky if she wound up with a porthole to peek out of on occasion.

Still, she didn't have the energy to question Miguel as he towed her along a wide polished wood hallway lined with gorgeous photographs of the sea and the occasional blown glass sculpture that made her think of waves inset in well-lit niches.

Everything was cozy and welcoming, with the exception of a single smoked glass door they passed. The modern monolith, complete with keypad entry, starkly contrasted the more traditional finishes. Sometime when her mind wasn't fuzzy with grief and fatigue, she might ask Miguel about it.

"Here we are." He paused in front of a wide door and entered a combination on the keypad. It seemed odd that he knew the code to her door, though she supposed he *did* own part of the ship. Maybe he had a master key code or something.

Except, when he opened it and ushered her inside the largest stateroom she'd ever seen on a ship, there were belongings on the shelves and a polished desk held an open notebook full of furious scribbles.

"Someone already lives here?" She'd shared housing before. Nothing as spacious or grand as this either. Except... She tried peeking around his broad shoulders to be sure. Yep, there was only one bed. A massive one at that.

"Yeah, me." Miguel crossed his arms, practically daring her to object.

Too tired to argue, she reached behind her for the door. One of his massive hands shot out, covering hers on the handle before she could yank it open.

"Banks has quarters prepared for you in the staff area, if you really want them. I think you'll be far more comfortable in my bed, though. Don't you?"

Miguel edged closer, causing her to take a step backward and then another, until her shoulders and ass bumped into the wall.

His heat and the enticing smell of ocean air on his skin weakened her objections. "Maybe."

The man didn't fight fair. He pressed his thigh between her legs, letting her ride the muscle there as he braced one forearm above her head, leaning in so their mouths nearly collided again.

Sabine licked her lips.

"That's right," he practically growled as his fingers brushed her hair behind her ear on one side. "Your hard nipples are telling me you want another shot at me as badly as I need to devour you. Why try to fight nature? Stay. Let me watch over you tonight. Tomorrow…we'll see where this goes."

"I should probably at least pretend to be a professional considering how gracious the Banks Foundation is being by sponsoring my research and granting me this opportunity." She didn't bother to deny their attraction. That would be a ridiculous argument.

Hell, it was all she could do to keep from putting her hands up to feel the solid muscles of his chest for herself. Maybe burrow into them and beg him to put his arms around her, sheltering her while she got some much needed rest.

It was a hard thing to admit for a woman who'd always prided herself on her independent streak. Except her whole soul felt bruised at the moment, and Miguel seemed plenty strong enough to take care of them both. Willing, too.

"We're adults. Who you sleep with is your business. If it makes you feel better, we can store your stuff downstairs for appearances, but we both know that'll be a waste of space." His confidence bordered on arrogance, yet somehow it still managed to make her squirm. In a good way. "Dishonest, too. I'm not the kind of man who sneaks around, fucking in the shadows. I'd be proud to have you stay with me, for everyone to know you're mine, if only for a little while. And I'll make damn sure you can say the same."

"Uh." Why couldn't she think of more reasons to turn down his proposal?

It wouldn't be the first spontaneous decision she'd made in her life. Nor the worst. Most likely.

"Besides, my suite has a jetted tub and the standard cabins only have showers. Big ass showers with fancy nozzles and shit, but still. You know you want my...bathtub." He wiggled his brows.

She groaned at the thought of soaking her aching body in steamy water. Five long cross-country and international flights in economy had threatened to permanently disfigure her. Booking her tickets last minute had meant she'd been the sucker jammed into the center seats. "Fine, you win."

"Always do." He nipped her bottom lip before pulling away to kiss her cheek. "Keep that in mind."

He didn't intimidate her.

In fact, part of her wished he hadn't stopped there. With a few quick movements, he could rip open his fly, shove down her jeans and panties, then help her forget anything except the pleasure he could undoubtedly give her. Yet he seemed true to his word. He wasn't going to manhandle her...tonight, anyway.

Sabine didn't want the guy to get too cocky. Plus, she thought she might test his self-control. See if he was as strong as he appeared. Experiments were her thing. So she stared straight at him as she walked the hem of her shirt up her torso. About the time she revealed her bra, which did a nice job of making the most of what she had, a muscle twitched in his jaw.

"If I knew you better, I might spank you for teasing me like that," he warned.

"Is that supposed to scare me?" It didn't. She'd often fantasized about finding a guy to play those kinds of games with. Only she'd never met one she thought could truly inspire her to hand herself over to like that.

Until now.

He had the potential to shake her up. Dangerous, this game she'd started playing.

That was what made it so fun. Where numbness had resided for days, he brought her back to life. It was a relief. Addictive, too.

Sabine dropped her shirt on the floor then shimmied out of her jeans. Her underwear, socks, and bra made a neat pile beside the rest of her clothes. Soon she wore only the necklace he'd put around her neck earlier. While his once-over may have originated with that item, it didn't stop there. She felt the sear of his gaze as it roamed lower and lower, remotely caressing her breasts before it focused on her center.

"You never have to be afraid of me or the things I'll do to you, *lindeza*. I'll make sure you enjoy every moment." If she hadn't been nude already, Miguel might have set her panties on fire with his thickening Brazilian accent. Would he talk to her like that while they fucked?

She shivered.

He admired her openly. "You should prepare yourself. It's going to be intense. I can tell already."

Sabine got the impression he didn't often wait to take what he desired. So she made the most of the anticipation, spinning to put her ass on display as she sashayed to his bathroom and bent over to turn on the hot, steamy water. Though she'd been drained minutes ago, even simple flirting with him invigorated her.

What would the real thing do for her?

"This is going to be the best assignment of my life." He made no apologies for staring at her, though he did intercede to keep her from lifting another finger. Miguel offered her his hand, helping her into the tub. He encouraged her to get comfortable while he brought her some body wash, lit a few candles, and queued up some nature sounds on his iPod to help her unwind. It reminded her of the time she'd spent in the field, her favorite part of her job. "When was the last time you ate?"

"Miguel, I don't even know what day it is right now," she answered honestly. "They gave us a chocolate-covered macadamia nut and some passion fruit juice on the flight in. Before that...couldn't say."

"Right." He grimaced. "I'm going to order some food for us. What would you like?"

There was a choice? And someone would bring it to them?

That impressed her more than the rest of the trappings she'd spied on their way to his private space. Standard fare on ships was whatever the hell the cook made and you were damn well happy to have it. Her hesitation and wide eyes must have been answer enough.

Miguel chuckled. "I know. I'm not quite used to this myself. It takes less time than you might imagine to get spoiled, though."

"I'm not sure how long I'm going to be around. Hopefully I can retrace Heinrich's steps pretty quick, before someone else does." She sank lower into the bubbles and crossed her arms over her nakedness as she tried for the millionth time to replay those seconds and zoom in on the shadow she'd seen in the corner of the screen. Had it been smoke, or the person she'd imagined at first?

"Hey, don't worry about that now. There will be plenty of time for work tomorrow and beyond. The best way you can help yourself prepare is to rest up and be at a hundred percent mentally before you get started, right?" He brushed his thumb over her shoulder. Though she had always felt comfortable in her own skin, she wished he would ditch his clothes, too.

Partially because she felt vulnerable. Mostly because she wanted to feast her eyes on what promised to be a spectacular body.

"Easy with that eye-fucking, tiger shark. Want me to serve myself up on a platter for you?" His smile made her sure room service would have an entirely different meaning if he was the one making the deliveries.

They might have ended up splashing water across the gorgeous marble floors, if her stomach hadn't growled loud enough to be heard over the running water.

"No more distractions, woman." Miguel asked again, "What can I get for you?"

"I'm guessing grilled fish is an option considering where we are, right?" She practically drooled as she considered eating something other than airport fare. "With some vegetables, maybe? It doesn't have to be anything fancy. Honestly, I'm probably not even going to taste it."

She yawned then. What she would really like was to shovel some sustenance into her face, swallow it in one giant gulp, then crash on the admittedly cloudlike bed she'd passed during her strut into the bathroom, which had apparently sapped the last of the charge in her internal batteries.

Though it was barely noon here, she wasn't going to be conscious much longer.

"Anything you don't like or are allergic to?"

"Nah. I'm pretty flexible." She shrugged, sighing as the warm water lapped over her collarbones.

"I think I'm going to like that about you." Miguel squeezed her hand. "I'll be right back."

The soft purr of his instructions to the chef reached her. Though she couldn't make out the words, she guessed his Brazilian accent was going to quickly become her favorite sound in the world. Maybe he would teach her some Portuguese so that she could listen to him speak more often.

As she considered where she'd started the day and how drastically things had changed the instant she'd met Miguel, she tried not to let guilt swamp her. Knowing how much Heinrich had cared for the kid he'd been, she had a sneaky suspicion he'd approve of her finding comfort in the man's arms. Even a temporary safe haven would be welcome at this turning point in her life.

Heinrich had often encouraged her to find a mate. Someone like Marta had been to him.

She closed her eyes at that, blocking out the pain that threatened to well up again as it had hundreds of times in the past week, and would thousands more in the coming years.

Sabine wasn't sure how long she floated there, buffeted by jets of blissful water. Long enough to doze off.

"Hey, not quite yet." Miguel shook her lightly when he returned. "I should have kept a closer eye on you knowing how tired you are. Jesus. Spend my life making sure tourists don't drown and I almost let a woman go under in my fucking tub."

Before she could reassure him she was fine, he had stripped, making it impossible to speak.

Instead, she beheld a living, breathing work of art finer than any she'd spotted during their trek to his cabin, or even had seen in Europe's most famous museums, which she'd loved to visit on weekends with Marta.

No fig leaf was going to cover *alllllllll* of that.

Sabine swallowed hard.

Miguel grinned. "You drooling over this dinner or what?"

She splashed him.

"Hey, be nice or I won't show you what Maria whipped up for you." He took a long skinny tray from where he'd leaned it up against the wall, and laid it across the tub. Then he set a covered silver platter in the center. Two wineglasses followed, along with a decanter of something that smelled expensive even from several feet away.

Two glasses?

Yep. Miguel stepped in on the other side of their makeshift table. When his lower half disappeared below the churning water, she aimed her attention at his cut chest and abs instead. Mmm. He looked good enough to eat.

The scent of lemon butter and fresh lobster pried her attention from his form momentarily. "Is that...?"

"Yep." He nodded, then unveiled the treat along with some rice pilaf, asparagus sticks, and a salad. "We caught them when we went spear fishing earlier. Dig in."

Sabine had already lunged for her silverware.

The first bite tasted divine. The warm, delicious food filled her empty belly.

"This is seriously the best thing I've ever put in my mouth." She hummed, then took another nibble.

"It'll only hold that record for another twelve hours or so." Miguel watched her lips, finally breaking his stare to glance down in the general vicinity of his cock, as if he were making the big guy a promise.

Laughter. She couldn't believe it was coming from her. In the midst of a crisis, she'd met a gorgeous, if crazy, man who ate lobster in a bathtub with her and cracked her up. Who was she to question the way life went sometimes?

Instead, they made the most of a shitty-but-not-so-shitty situation. After she'd finished stuffing herself, she had no hope of extending her get-to-know-you session with Miguel, no matter how many more questions she had for the guy.

Her eyelids grew heavy.

Of course he noticed.

With a single graceful motion, he stood, allowing the water to sluice from his magnificent body. He tucked the empty plates and glasses to one side then stepped out, quickly drying himself off before holding out a hand to her.

Sabine took it, stepping over the high side of the tub. She walked into the fluffy towel he held out to wrap her in. She allowed him to take control, ensuring she didn't skip any of even the most basic tasks she was incapable of performing for herself at the moment. It was odd, and sort of comforting, to let him care for her in this way.

A way she'd never allowed another man to do.

And when he lifted her into his arms and carried her to bed, she didn't protest. He placed her near the center of the mattress then climbed in behind her, drawing the covers up and hitting some button on a control panel nearby. Room-darkening shades blocked the lovely ocean view and plunged them into artificial darkness.

The feel of another human being, skin on skin, grounded her. She turned toward him and wrapped herself around every part of him she could reach. He did the same, entwining them thoroughly. His fingertips glided up and down her spine. For a few seconds, she counted the slow, solid beats of his heart from where her ear pressed to his chest. It must have hypnotized her.

That was the only reason she could think of to explain why she blurted, "I should have been there with him."

She'd thought about it over and over non-stop since the moment her world had blown to smithereens.

"*Lindeza*, no. Then you both might have been lost." Miguel hugged her a little tighter. "What good could you have done against an explosion, huh?"

She recalled the masked man she thought she had seen. Ridiculous, right?

Sabine shrugged. "At least he wouldn't have doubted my loyalties. It's just that after I graduated from his program, I needed to fly solo for a couple years. Earn my own way before latching on to his success like some kind of remora feeding off its host shark, you know? I had lots of offers for grants to study pretty much whatever I wanted. Including one from Heinrich. I should have taken it. My ego kept us apart, and now I'll never get to team up with him again."

She bit her lower lip, trying to squish it to keep it from trembling.

"I'm sorry you won't have that chance." Miguel rocked her gently then murmured against her temple, "But you must be pretty fucking smart and great at your job to have institutions begging for you like that. Heinrich must have been so proud of you."

That was all it took.

There was no protecting herself against the onslaught of grief. Sabine clung to Miguel's shoulders as if he was the *Divemaster*'s anchor while the storm of pain raged around them. He'd accidentally mashed one of her most sensitive spots. No matter how often Heinrich had praised her accomplishments, Sabine had tried to work harder to deserve his praise.

In the end, that drive had kept her away from her second father in the final days of his life.

She would never see him again. Never have the chance to tell him how much she loved him.

Sabine bawled. She cried until she could hardly breathe, despite Miguel's soothing litany of calming nonsense. He never once let go.

Miguel held her as she sobbed, told her it was okay. Even if he lied, she appreciated the comfort he bestowed. And when the anguish had finally snuffed itself out, leaving her empty, she sagged against his side.

"Better?" he asked.

She nodded a tiny bit to keep the pounding headache she felt coming on from developing before she could fall asleep. Which she planned to do as soon as she set the record straight.

"Just so you know, I'm not the sort of girl who blubbers over dumb shit." Sabine sniffled as she glared at him from eyes that must be puffy and red. Boner-killer material for sure.

"Cool, because I don't have a lot of experience here." His lips twisted into a wry smile. "I mean, I'm not the kind of guy who women usually come to with a broken heart."

She winced at that. "No, I bet you're the one who does the breaking."

He blinked, seeming to actually consider what she'd said. "I hope not."

Sabine couldn't believe he'd be so oblivious. She didn't intend to be one of his tragedies. A fling with him would be spectacular. A highlight to balance out the poisonous darkness that threatened to seep into the hole Heinrich had left inside her.

It also wouldn't last forever.

She'd finish her job here. Or he'd grow bored. They'd both move on.

At least she knew that going in. Like all good things, including the very best of people in her life, this too would go away.

Sabine hadn't been ready for Heinrich to leave, but she'd make damn sure she was prepared to let go of Miguel when their time ran out. Until then, she snuggled deeper into his hold. "Miguel?"

"Yeah, *lindeza*?"

"Heinrich would have been awfully proud of you, too." She kissed his neck then. "Thank you."

He went still, but didn't respond. His fingers idly traced the line of his necklace around her throat as he considered what she'd said. Hopefully he believed her, because she didn't have even a speck of energy left to reiterate her certainty.

Unconsciousness dragged her deep under.

∽ SIX ∾

S abine stretched, wallowing in the softness that enveloped her. Well, other than that one warm, solid, hunk of...*manmeat*?

Her fingers flexed, unconsciously kneading muscle of some variety.

She blinked. Yep, that was definitely a ripped abdomen pillowing her head. Looking up, the blurry outline of an inky-haired man with eyes as bright as a turquoise sea gradually came into focus. He watched over her from where his merman-worthy shoulders rested against a padded leather headboard. Miguel.

"Hey," she croaked, her mouth dry. How long had she been unconscious? It felt like a while. Sunlight still limned the blinds covering his stateroom windows, though.

"Good morning," he murmured as he stroked her hair with smooth, repetitive motions. It made her wonder if he'd gotten some practice doing it over the past several hours. Knowing he'd guarded her while she'd been dead to the world stirred something inside her.

Gratitude, and more primal emotions along with it.

True, she had just met the man. But they'd already shared experiences more intimate than those she generally indulged in with long-term lovers. Grieving, bathing, sleeping, reminiscing about shared acquaintances, and even the meal they'd eaten together had been so personal it made their connection seem real and deeper than it could possibly be, given that she'd spent less than a day in his company while awake.

Right?

The illusions of security and permanence could be treacherous. Especially when cast by a stranger. Doubly so if she hadn't had a lifetime of experience in temporary relationships—romantic or otherwise. Fortunately, she did. So she allowed herself to see where their instant chemistry might take them.

It was then that his greeting fully sank in.

"Morning?" She glanced around for a clock.

"Yeah. You were really out of it. Have to say that's a first. Women don't usually spend so much time in my bed actually asleep. Or if they do, it's *after* I've fucked them senseless."

"Now that sounds like a cruise activity I could enjoy. Where do I sign up?" Sabine's hand began to wander along the inside of his leg toward his thick, hardening shaft. He made more than a handful while barely roused. This could be a *big* bonus to her time onboard. Something to help her de-stress.

The instant she curled her fingers around him, measuring him, he tugged her upward, thwarting her plans to demonstrate her appreciation for his very warm welcome.

Miguel captured her mouth with his and showed her again that no matter how bold she grew with him, he wouldn't be unsettled. Neither did he let her wrest control from him with the hint of a hand job or find his determination to seduce her wavering due to the proximity of her lips to his dick. It would take a lot more than that to derail his alpha tendencies.

Challenge accepted.

Meeting her kiss for kiss, he palmed her ass and situated her in his lap as he pleased.

Sabine sighed when her thighs spread around his torso and her knees sank into the plush bedding. The silky brush of skin on skin had her rubbing against Miguel like the harbor seals had done to the kelp in Monterey Bay. When he nudged the seam of her smile, she admitted his tongue between her lips.

Subtle upward thrusts of his hips tucked his still firming hard-on against her mound.

When she tried to lift herself a little more, high enough to put his dick where she really wanted it, he gripped her tighter.

He separated their faces long enough to breathe, "Wait, *lindeza*—"

"What does that mean? You called me that yesterday." Inquisitive by nature, she couldn't help but wonder despite the heat of his embrace or the increasing urgency of her arousal.

"Beautiful. You are. Extraordinarily so." The conviction with which he said it melted her insides. It would have melted her panties too, if she'd been wearing any. Appealing to him couldn't be a bad thing. Not when he looked at her with such hungry eyes.

So she rewarded him with another caress of her mouth over his, this time nipping his lower lip. She didn't know where the compulsion to do it came from. It seemed he brought out something new in her that none of her previous partners had. Their unique combination fascinated her.

Miguel groaned, then ratcheted up the intensity of their kisses. She buried her fingers in his thick hair, pawing at his skull while he did the same to her ass. His thumbs hooked around her hip bones kept her from gliding along the length of his cock. Too bad, she probably could have gotten herself off with the friction of his blunt tip prodding her clit alone.

Well, that along with the way her breasts felt as they dragged against his chest, and the decadent things he was doing to her mouth. Her tongue had certainly given guys plenty of pleasure before. Never in her life had it been the source of so much for her. Miguel sucked on it, raked his teeth over it lightly, and swirled his own around it, nearly making her pant into his mouth.

If he could do that with a not-so-simple kiss, what could he do if he engaged the rest of his body?

When she was breathless and nearly dizzy from making out with him, she paused to suck in some much needed oxygen.

Her fingers ached from where she'd unknowingly dug them into his powerful shoulders.

"Sorry," she muttered as she unclamped them, rubbing out the dents she'd left behind. He seemed to enjoy her caresses or at least indulged them. Good thing, since she'd discovered she loved touching him. Smooth, ultra-tan skin wrapped around warm, supple muscles.

It felt so good, she couldn't stop running her hands along his shoulders and upper arms.

Miguel flashed her a lopsided grin. "Got carried away for a second. That's what I wanted to say. It seems like you and I together could get kind of rowdy. Still think this is a good idea now that you've slept on it?"

"It's probably not wise," she acknowledged.

His grip loosened.

She speared her fingers into his hair and angled his face so he could read the truth in her gaze. "That doesn't mean I don't want to do it anyway. Kind of like when you're stuffed but you order dessert because it looks so damn delicious; how could you not?"

Sabine licked her lips, her eyelids drooping at the taste of him lingering there. Yes, scrumptious.

"I've always had a sweet tooth myself." He grinned as he lunged forward, taking her to her back on the bed as he hovered over her on straight-locked arms. "I have a feeling you could finally satisfy me."

Though his bulk and strength made it clear how exposed she was lying beneath him, his admission gave her power. What exactly had he been searching for yet not finding?

Who didn't want to be that elusive thing for a man like him?

She certainly hoped she could be, at least temporarily. It seemed like they'd both be making the best of what time they had together.

Sabine moaned when Miguel kissed along the column of her neck. Instinctively, she stretched her chin up, granting him better access. When the edge of his teeth raked along her pulse, she shivered. She'd never had a man like this—raw and animalistic.

No polite lover here.

Thank God.

By the time Miguel had wandered to her breasts, licking and suckling one while his hand worked its magic on the other, she had stopped thinking rationally and had given herself over completely to feeling. It was rare that she was able to turn off the side of her brain that collected information and facts, cataloging even her own responses during sex.

For the first time in years, she found herself lost in the moment.

Data be damned.

Leaving her worries behind was a pleasure in itself. Relief enhanced her desire.

When Miguel slithered between her thighs, levering them far apart so that his wide shoulders fit between them, he nuzzled her stomach. The stubble peppering his cheeks rasped lightly over her sensitive skin, making her writhe beneath him. He chuckled, then inhaled deeply, as if memorizing her scent before burying his face in her core.

There was nothing delicate about his approach. Nothing tentative or unsure.

He dove right in and started blowing her mind with bold swipes of his tongue that collected the moisture slickening her folds.

"*Yes.*" Sabine threw her head back as one hand flew to his shoulder. Not so she could keep him there against his will—mostly to brace herself during the onslaught of passion. Though part of her was terrified he might stop before she'd finished coming all over his face because that was certainly where this was headed.

It wasn't going to take very long either.

The man deserved an award for pussy-eating.

And when his fingers circled her opening, zeroing in on the best angle for entrance, she cried out his name.

"Mmm," he purred against her flesh, as if he liked the way it sounded bursting from her lips.

Good thing since he had her screaming for him over and over when he inserted first one finger then another, working her open as he continued to flick his tongue across her clit precisely the way she preferred.

"Miguel!" This time it was a warning, with maybe a hint of a plea.

He correctly read the urgency in her shout, spurring her over the finish line with the press of his skilled fingers on some amazing place inside her.

Sabine shattered. She lifted up in an orgasmic crunch so she could watch him revel in her pleasure. It only made her hotter to see how devoted he was to bringing her ecstasy, knowing soon she would do the same for him.

When she crested the wave of rapture and began to fall back to reality, she collapsed on the bed, marveling at the effects of the host of endorphins that flooded her system. Biology and chemistry held true sorcery sometimes. A rush like this could become a habit.

Before she could dip too much from her high, Miguel rejoined her. Face to face, he smiled as he took in her flushed cheeks and dilated pupils. For all the gentleness in his expression, he couldn't mask the furious desire beneath it.

Neither could he hide the heat and weight of his rock-hard cock against her thigh.

"Fuck me," she practically begged.

"I'd like to take the time to do this properly." Miguel sighed. "Somehow I don't think you're going to let me distract you for much longer, though."

Sabine winced at the reminder of her duties and how she wasn't doing them—until he put on a show for her, retrieving a condom from beneath his pillow, tearing it open, then rolling it down his impressive length fast enough that she knew he'd had a lot of practice with the maneuver.

Before she could make some smartass remark, he'd returned and notched his covered head at her opening, a mere twitch of a muscle from joining them for the first of what she hoped would be many times.

"This will have to do for now." He kissed her, blanking out every thought except the pressure of the tip of his cock embedded in her pussy, on the cusp of entering. "Later I'll show you what I'm really capable of and give you what you deserve. As much pleasure as you can handle. I promise, *lindeza*."

As he rumbled her new favorite word, he advanced, spearing himself a few inches farther into her. He stretched her wide.

Damn, the man had a fat cock. Not that she was complaining.

Relaxing, or trying to, she admitted him deeper within her body each time they rocked together.

"That's good. Let me in." He crooned to her in a mix of English and Portuguese that she didn't have to understand literally to comprehend.

Sexy talk was sexy in any language. Maybe even more so when she relied on his expression and inflection to interpret the sentiment.

Miguel distracted her from the initial discomfort of her body learning to accommodate his with a flurry of kisses and caresses. He rolled his hips in a smooth, rhythmic pattern that guaranteed he would make one hell of a dance partner, too.

For now, his qualifications as a fuck buddy were far more important to her.

Sabine hissed when he surged forward, his trunk meeting hers finally as she held his entire shaft within her. His balls knocked against her, making her want to scream out some primitive victory.

"That's right. Take all of me." He pressed against her, making quite the impression with his dick.

In fact, she couldn't wait for him to pull out some simply so he could reintroduce them, though nothing might ever match the awe of this very first time she found out what it was like to be filled completely by him...or anyone else. No man had ever imprinted himself on her—in her—like this before.

Not only because of his incredible cock. Or even because he knew how to use it so damn well. It was more than that. His need matched hers in a way she couldn't quite analyze at the moment.

Didn't plan to either.

Sabine rocked her hips, first away, then back. He didn't need any more encouragement than that. "So slick. Tight and hot. You're ready for me, huh?"

She didn't bother to answer. Instead, she repeated her motion, groaning when she couldn't make as big of a difference as she would have liked.

"Don't worry, *lindeza*." He kissed her one last time before getting serious about the ride he was about to give her. "I'm gonna do the work for you. All you have to do is hold on. If you can."

She might have thought his cockiness was exclusively bravado if he hadn't made good on his pledge right then. Miguel didn't bother with a gradual ramp up. Instead, he listened to the demands of her body, fucking her exactly as she needed. Hard, fast, and thoroughly. Without restraint.

She took pride in knowing she could handle the full intensity of a man like him.

Hell, that she could match it.

Sabine planted her feet on the mattress, bracing herself to accept the impact of his pelvis against hers. She stared into his eyes as he lunged over her, withdrawing until the ring of muscles at her opening strangled his fat head, before plunging fully within her.

Even when she clamped around him, clasping his shuttling shaft, he maintained his pace.

If anything, he increased the tempo of his thrusts.

"Yes. Like that." He ordered, "Squeeze my cock with that pretty pussy. Come around it. Let me feel how much you love it when I fuck you deep and hard like this. Take me under with you. Do it. Now."

As if she needed any additional incentives, he reached between them to roll her pebbled nipple between his thumb and forefinger. The extra stimulation proved impossible to resist.

Or was it his command that tipped her over the edge?

Either way, she obeyed.

Sabine screamed as the most powerful orgasm of her life overtook her. The shimmer of gathering rapture blazed and spread like a firework inside her, illuminating each of the dark corners she'd been afraid to acknowledge in the past.

Miguel wouldn't allow her to shrink away from her nature.

Instead, he embraced it, and encouraged her to do the same. "Ah. Fuck, yes. You're even more gorgeous when you're coming for me. Shattering around my cock like this."

His praise set off another round of spasms. This time he proved he wasn't immune to her reactions either.

"I'm going to fill this condom for you." He grunted as he slammed into her pussy a few more times, extending her ecstasy. "My balls have never ached so bad in my life."

Sabine hadn't realized how much of a turn on it could be for a man to express his desires so openly and honestly. She gladly accepted each of his wild penetrations, happy to return even a fraction of the bliss he'd given her.

The tensing of his jaw gave him away.

Sabine clenched around him.

He cursed, then shouted her name as he jackhammered into her. With each slap of his flesh against hers, he growled and shuddered, making her certain he was doing exactly as he'd said he would, pouring his lust into the thin latex reservoir between them.

For a wild moment, she wished she could feel the heat of his release marking her deep inside.

Though no one else might know, she was sure she'd feel the brand he'd left with his possession every time she had sex for the rest of her life. How could anything else be as good as this?

When, finally, they finished jerking against each other, he rolled to his back. Cradling her against his chest, he murmured to her in Portuguese until she regained the ability to think anything other than, *Holy shit. Holy shit. Holy shit.*

"Hey there, *lindeza*." He smiled when her eyelids fluttered open and she caught him observing her as they recovered. "Doing okay?"

"Uh huh." She nodded, rubbing her cheek against the slightly damp plane of his chest.

How had he leveled her completely yet hardly broken a sweat?

"Don't look so proud of yourself." She reached up and tweaked his nipple, causing him to laugh and capture her hand. He brought her fingers to his lips and nibbled her knuckles before placing a kiss over the mild sting.

"Truth is, I'm kind of embarrassed." He shook his head. "I don't think I've ever come so quickly. Especially not when I'm trying hard to impress."

"If that's your idea of a premature ejaculation, I can't wait to see what you consider a marathon fuck."

"Give me five minutes and I'll be happy to show you." He brushed the pad of his thumb over her bottom lip. "Less time if you keep looking at me like my dick is your new favorite toy."

"As tempting as that may be, hiding under the covers won't solve my problems or find Heinrich's cure." She winced. How could she have let herself be distracted so easily?

Oh, right, Miguel *did* have a stellar cock and the skill to put it to good use. Not exactly an everyday occurrence when it came to guys. At least she tried to convince herself it was only his equipment that had aroused her so thoroughly. Anything else was too reckless.

"Can't blame a man for trying." He kissed the side of her neck. "I'll be more convincing tonight."

Sabine hoped he held off until then because she could only muster so much willpower when her pussy cheered for a repeat performance.

Damn. She sighed, frowning as she wondered if she'd gotten herself into more trouble than she could handle.

"Hey, I'm mostly teasing." He kissed her lips softly then climbed from bed, flashing his perfect ass on his way into the bathroom. "We can be in your lab and working thirty minutes from now including a stop in the dining room for some breakfast. I'll try to focus on something other than your sweet pussy for a few hours at least."

"Gee, thanks." Okay, so she liked knowing she appealed to a man as fine as Miguel.

"That's going to require an incredible amount of restraint on my part, for the record." When he turned toward her slightly, she could see his rejuvenating cock, already half-hard.

If only she didn't feel the weight of Heinrich's legacy she might have done something about it. After the spectacular way Miguel had gone down on her before giving her the fuck of a lifetime, she figured she owed him some payback.

"Tonight." She nodded.

"Deal. Now get in here and let me jack off to the sight of your soapy tits jiggling in my shower or I won't even make it to lunchtime before stealing you away for another quickie."

She laughed, but he didn't seem to be joking. Not about classifying the best sex of her life as a mere quickie, or about his need to come again so soon either.

The hand stroking his cock was serious as shit.

What the hell had she gotten herself into with him? Something spectacular, and a little scary, if she was being honest. Ah well, there'd be time to worry about that later.

She wondered if he would come faster if she played with herself while under the balmy spray that rained on her from a half-dozen different showerheads.

He wasn't the only one charged up by their unexpected connection.

Though she didn't have a baseline to compare his reactions to, her gut told her that her hypothesis had been correct when neither of them lasted more than a couple minutes before climaxing while on display for the other.

In her case, it was a clear result.

Miguel affected her like no one had before. He made her crave things she couldn't have. Do things she shouldn't.

At a critical time in her life, she couldn't afford a distraction that huge. As they dressed and prepared to head out, uncertainty crept past her receding rapture. Had she fucked this up before she'd even gotten started?

Maybe this afternoon she'd take Banks up on those staff quarters after all. Just in case, she tidied her belongings, tucking them into the single suitcase she'd brought.

How would Miguel take the news?

"Don't even think it." He seemed to read her mind when he took her hand and guided her from the room before she could finish zipping her bag. "There's nowhere to run on this ship even if you wanted to. And we both know you don't. Not really."

Of course, he was right.

SEVEN

After wolfing down an assortment of fresh mango, papaya, and pineapple along with a bowl of granola, Sabine drained two glasses of blackberry mint lemonade. Then she toyed with her spoon, itching to go, as Miguel devoured yet another helping of eggs and bacon.

The man could eat.

She was pretty sure she knew how he worked that energy off, too. Between swimming and fucking, he had earned those golden muscles giving his soft cotton T-shirt so much definition.

"You're antsy to get started. I can be done here." He wiped his mouth on his napkin before taking one last gulp of water.

"No, don't rush. Maybe I should go ahead, though. I feel like I wasted a whole day." She stared out the window hardly admiring the gorgeous scenery, wondering how she could have let attraction—even one as strong as the one compelling her toward Miguel—derail her.

He grimaced. "You weren't any good for anything yesterday. You had to recharge your brainiac batteries."

As he was in the middle of being practical and shit, a tall blond man as fit and *nearly* as sexy as Miguel dropped into an empty chair beside them at a long, polished table on one of the upper decks.

"I guess I don't blame you for disappearing yesterday." Their breakfast buddy slapped Miguel on the shoulder. "Well done, stealing her away for yourself before she had a chance to meet *me*."

Sabine laughed, flattered rather than embarrassed given his obvious approval of their affair.

"I'm not an idiot." Miguel threw a croissant at his friend. "Don't you be one either. She's gorgeous and she's *mine*, so make sure that flirting is as far as you dare go if you want to keep your balls attached."

The man nodded subtly at the warning before turning to her with a brilliant smile. He offered his hand. "I'm Tosin, one of the divemasters on the *Divemaster*."

She wiped her hand on her linen napkin before shaking his, awed by how his fingers engulfed hers with a steady yet careful grasp. "One of the owners, you mean? Miguel and Archer's partner, right?"

He shrugged. "I guess so. Still feels kind of weird. I'm a lot simpler than that, really."

"Simple is right," Miguel grumbled when Tosin held on to her palm a little too long for his liking.

Sabine withdrew, her cheeks heating at the effect these guys had on her. What was wrong with her? Or was it them?

Their bond shone through in the way they seemed to know the other's thoughts and how they read each other's body language. Tosin even stole a few bites off Miguel's plate, which his friend didn't seem to mind in the least. Exactly how close were they? How much had they shared?

Illicit fantasies sprang to life. Ones where she found herself sandwiched between them.

She blinked.

Trying to get her mind back to safer ground she asked, "Is your accent Danish?"

"Close." Tosin smiled. "I'm originally from the Netherlands. Haven't been home in ages, though. I heard you studied in Germany."

"Yes." She nodded, trying to ignore the sting in her eyes.

"I'm sorry about your mentor."

Both Miguel and Tosin covered one of her hands then, squeezing lightly. Miguel didn't glare at his friend for offering comfort, so she gladly accepted it.

Sabine swallowed hard, "Thank you."

"I didn't mean to eavesdrop. I did hear you talking when I sat down, though. Don't worry about yesterday. As much as I hate to admit it, Miguel is right for once. You must have been exhausted. Besides, it took most of the day for Banks to wave his fairy godfather wand and turn part of the dive bay into a lab for you." He promised, "You couldn't have gotten started until today anyway. Banks is good, but even he's human. I think. Pretty sure."

"I owe you so much." She looked to Miguel especially then. He'd given her something equally as precious, helped ground her when she needed to be at her best academically. "I don't know how I'll ever repay you."

"I bet he's got a few ideas about that." Tosin broke the heavy atmosphere, causing her to snort.

"Tosin..." Miguel growled.

"Seriously, though, it's part of what we do around here. Thanks to Archer and his inheritance. We're trying to make a difference in the world. What we do is minor. You...well, you have the capability to make an enormous impact. However we can facilitate that, we'd love to be a part of it." Tosin stood then, grabbing one last slice of bacon off Miguel's plate. "So I'll let you get to it. I just wanted to say hello before I set up for the next group of divers."

Sabine had nearly forgotten about the other guests Marta had explained would be onboard, focused on her own mission.

"Thank you. For everything." Sabine went with her gut, reaching up to pull him into a one-armed hug, which he returned with interest.

"No problem. If there's anything I can do to help out let me know. Even if it's kicking this cocksplatter's ass for you when he fucks up. See ya later!" Tosin hustled out then before Miguel could retaliate with anything other than the dual middle fingers he flashed.

She balled up her napkin and put her hands in her lap, trying not to fidget.

"Come on, I'm finished." Miguel stood and scooted her chair away from the table like a proper gentleman. A complete turnabout from the savage he'd proven he could be in bed. Fortunately, both sides of him appealed to her.

He laced their fingers together as he guided her toward the stern of the megayacht then down a set of winding teak stairs. As they curved, she caught sight of a crescent-shaped speck of land jutting from the open ocean. She whipped her head in the opposite direction, spying the southern coast of Maui, then back. "Is that Molokini?"

Miguel didn't even have to look in the direction she lifted her chin toward. There was no mistaking the islet. Especially since nothing but miles and miles of empty Pacific stretched beyond that. "Yep. We were hoping to take the guests snorkeling and diving at a bunch of the sites within the crater, depending on your plans and whether you're ready to begin your research this quickly. It's notorious for its insane visibility and provides a wide range of difficulties that will make it ideal for the groups with various levels of experience already onboard."

"Oh, that will be perfect!" Sabine felt the first flutters of excitement in her belly. This was what she'd trained for. What she'd dreamed of. Though she never would have hoped for these circumstances, the thought of making a breakthrough discovery still thrilled her. "Marta and I were searching for vessels in range of this area. She found you guys and reached out to the Banks Foundation about the possibility of coming onboard because we know this was Heinrich's last stop on his collection trip, which wrapped about three weeks earlier than expected. He'd never done that before. I believe he quit looking when he found whatever it was that had him going bananas. I didn't realize you were already *here*, though. I'm glad I'm not pulling you off course."

"It wouldn't matter. Wherever you need us to go, we'll be there." Miguel squeezed her hand, infusing his strength into their connection.

He ushered her onto the dive platform and she stutter stepped. He was right there to steady her, keeping himself between her and the ocean lapping at the hull. "Wow."

"I know." He chuckled. "I still can't believe we get to work here."

She looked around at the pristine gear, so neatly organized across the spacious bay. It had everything you could wish for, more than she'd ever had the luxury of diving with before on a research vessel. Damn.

When she'd picked her jaw up off the decking, Miguel led her to a nook tucked into the back corner. It looked like it had been an open-air study area that they'd enclosed with tinted aquamarine glass especially for her. The space inside wasn't the largest she'd ever seen, but it was perfect. Whiteboards, centrifuges, microscopes, test tubes, chemical lockers…you name it, they had it. *She* had it at her disposal. Every essential and even a few perks she hadn't had in her Monterey research facility.

Including a man who was turning out to be the most capable assistant on Earth.

"Will this be okay?" Miguel asked her. "Say the word and I'm sure Banks can arrange for anything else you need. Seriously, just let me know and we'll make it happen."

Sabine wiped moisture from the corner of one eye. Who said there weren't good people left in the world?

She turned to him and flung her arms around his neck. When he caught her, she added her legs to the full body hug.

"Wait until Banks gets *his* thank-you kiss," Tosin teased from the doorway where he leaned against the frame. Archer and Waverly laughed softly from behind him. "It'll probably be the highlight of his year."

"It would indeed," Banks said entirely too primly for anyone to keep a straight face.

Sabine unwound herself from Miguel and trotted to Banks. She went onto her tiptoes to buss his cheek noisily, causing him to beam as he patted her back lightly.

"Thank you so much," she whispered.

"You're very welcome, dear." He straightened the black ruffles around the neckline of her crocheted cover-up, which hid a modest one-piece suit beneath. His stare caught on her necklace. "That's beautiful."

"I think so, too." She smiled. "Miguel made it. When he was a boy."

"Really?" Banks shifted his assessing gaze to the man in question, who only shrugged. "It makes you wonder sometimes, doesn't it, if there's truly such a thing as fate."

"I'm a believer," Waverly said, without taking her stare from Archer.

He rested his forehead on hers and smiled softly before murmuring, "Me too."

Some other time, Sabine would have to ask Miguel about their story.

"So where do you want to start?" he asked her, drawing her thoughts back to the present.

She drew a deep breath then let it out as she studied the ceiling of her brand spanking new laboratory. "While I was flying here, I reread every email Heinrich sent me during his collection trip and the follow up experiments at his research center. I'm starting to think he was trying to tell me more than I realized at the time. I should have listened closer."

Miguel tucked one of her unruly curls behind her ear. "Let's focus on going forward. He wouldn't want you to beat yourself up. You didn't have all the information then that you do now. What did you figure out?"

"There was one letter he sent, after they'd been in this area for about two weeks. He'd seemed increasingly frustrated, which wasn't like him at all. Then one day the tone was totally different. He said, 'Sometimes you fail to notice the obvious when you're trying too hard or making things more complex than they need to be. What you're searching for can be right in front of you. Until you change the way you look at things—blind yourself to what you think you know and dig a little deeper—you might never see it.'"

"What the hell do you think that means?" Tosin rubbed his temple.

She took a deep breath. "As best I can figure, he was letting me know that what he found originated from something ordinary. Probably something he or other marine biologists have studied countless times. As counterintuitive as it seems, I think I want to dive here and collect samples from the most common species around. It could be that he processed them differently than usual, or maybe that something about this location makes them slightly dissimilar—enough to have far-reaching implications—from other forms. Maybe no one noticed sooner because they dismissed those possibilities based on previous results, instead of on the facts alone. I need to blind myself to what I think I know, and start from scratch with the basics."

"It's as good a theory as any, I suppose." Banks hummed his approval as Tosin, Archer, and Waverly nodded in agreement.

"Waverly and I can tell you from experience that assuming you know what's going on instead of questioning everything can really steer you wrong," Archer admitted.

"A solid lesson for life as well as this experiment," Miguel agreed. She wondered what parts of himself he was reexamining at the moment. Could their meeting have shaken him up also?

"So you'll go with me? Point out stuff you see all the time around here? Help me collect and tag everything while we're waiting for my tissue samples to arrive? Run tests and track results once they get here?" Sabine asked Miguel. Having him by her side beneath the waves would keep her level. Another pair of hands in the lab would be invaluable, too.

Already she trusted him. If his SCUBA skills were anywhere near as good as his fucking abilities, she had seriously won the assistant lottery.

"Hell yeah. Let's go diving." Miguel grinned. "I can't wait to go down with you."

For the first time since the explosion that had rocked her foundation from across the world, Sabine felt confident that she could do her mentor justice and complete his research. With this kind of unwavering support, how could she not?

Heinrich's death—no, his *life*—had to mean something.

If she could give this to the world in his name, It would.

She nodded at Miguel. "I'm ready."

"I know." He kissed her, right there in front of his honorary family. She didn't pull away either.

EIGHT

TWO WEEKS LATER

Sabine had massively underestimated Miguel. Though she considered herself a seasoned diver, he took things to another level. A true expert, he was mesmerizing to watch, or might have been if she wasn't attempting to focus on the job at hand. All three divemasters had complimented her proficiency after joining them beneath the surface at one time or another recently. She had nothing on them.

In addition to his aptitude with the equipment, constant vigilance for safety issues, effortless buoyancy control, and eyes as sharp as a shark's for spotting creatures or coral specimens she'd have zipped right past underwater, Miguel had stamina that would put that guy who had swum across the Adriatic Sea without flippers to shame.

He dove with her every morning, leading two- or three-tank collecting expeditions that crisscrossed the reef inside the horseshoe of the Molokini Crater, leaving no stone or coral head unturned. It didn't matter what the conditions were like, or how tired he might have been from swimming like a fish—a gorgeous, sleek, and powerful fish—assisting her in the lab every afternoon and evening, then fucking her damn near into a coma each night.

Sabine had never been as exhausted, or as sated, as she was right then.

If they had only made even a hint of progress toward locating Heinrich's mysterious cure, she would be in heaven. Instead, guilt corroded her guts when her laptop made the triple-chirp associated with an incoming call on her video chat software.

Only one person used it these days.

And Sabine had been ducking those notifications for a while.

"Want me to answer that for you?" Miguel asked as he spied her gloved hands and the latest concoction she was about to inject into a cancerous tissue specimen. If she introduced any contaminants during the process, she could invalidate her test, assuming that this one would be any more fruitful than the thousands of others she'd prepared over the past two weeks.

"Nah. I'll call her back some other time." She looked at her hands, unable to meet his gaze.

"Is this Heinrich's wife?" He peered at the icon on her screen.

Sabine nodded, unable to speak around the lump in her throat.

"Are you dodging her?" he asked.

She lifted a single shoulder.

That was all it took. Miguel hit connect even as she cried out, "Don't!"

"I knew you were avoiding me." Marta *tsked*, clearly having heard her shout. "Not like you. Especially since you're the only family I have left in the world, girl."

Toss another guilt log on the fire, Sabine thought. Even worse, Banks had peeked into the laboratory, probably because he'd heard her holler, too.

Miguel shocked her by coming to her defense. He disarmed Marta with a wave and one of the blinding full-on smiles he usually reserved for Sabine. "Hello Mrs. Geld. I'm so sorry for your loss. Please understand that *our* girl is hurting, too. Although we both know she shouldn't, she feels like crap because we haven't had any luck with her research yet."

Was it that obvious? She thought she'd given her best to Miguel, genuinely enjoying their time together, and feeling even shittier because of it. How could she find something to be so damn happy about when Marta's world had fallen apart? It wasn't fair, and it wasn't right.

"*Our* girl? *Ich glaub mein Schwein pfeift!* Who is this handsome *boy*, Sabine?" Marta asked with a slightly harsher than normal German accent. The woman was direct, something Sabine usually appreciated. Right now, though, she wished she wasn't such an open book. How could she explain when she didn't know where she and Miguel stood herself?

The sex was great. Like, better than Marta's infamous black forest cake and four birthdays rolled into one. But when her time here was over, that would go away, too. They hadn't made each other any promises. It would be pointless, as they each would go their own way to keep saving the world with the tools they had. Their paths had crossed temporarily. Eventually they would diverge again.

Sabine opened her mouth but closed it again when Miguel responded for her. "My name is Miguel Torres. I'm a divemaster here. Your husband was a great influence on me when I was younger. A friend, and an inspiration."

"I knew it!" Marta softened immediately, her suggestion of a frown perking up into a smile. "I hope you don't mind that I poked around about the co-owners of the ship my Sabine would be spending her time on. I read your bio and the articles that have been circulating about you and your partners since the formation of the Divemaster Project. About where you're from, how you're self-made, and your impressive goals. Your name matched and I could see the resemblance to the photo Heinrich had of the two of you. After all this time, I hoped it might really be you. My husband was a good judge of character, son. He talked about you often. Remembered you fondly."

Afraid the moisture gathering in her eyes might leak out and ruin her work, Sabine finished up what she had been doing, then set the timer. When it went off, she should be able to detect some progress, *if* the solution she'd prepped and infused made any difference whatsoever. She peeled off her gloves then approached her laptop warily, as if it were a stonefish out to stab her with its poisonous spikes.

Having her two worlds collide like this made it all too real.

Miguel wasn't a figment of her imagination, some dream concocted by her subconscious to help her make it through one of the roughest parts of her life. He was real. Here. With her. But he wouldn't always be. Somehow, having Marta meet him—know that he existed—would make the loss more profound once he was no longer part of her life.

Banks edged closer, and Tosin joined them, too. They must have looked ridiculous, crunched together in front of the screen. Marta was magnetic like that, though. She drew people in, and made them listen.

"That means a lot. Thank you." Miguel put his arm around Sabine, tucking her against his heat and strength. Subconsciously, she toyed with his necklace, which became more precious to her every day. Though she should have pulled away, stood on her own, she couldn't bring herself to do it.

Not when she had to admit her failures to the one person who cared the most about what she was supposed to be concentrating on here. Sabine blurted, "I haven't found anything, Marta. I'm sorry. We're almost out of samples, too. I thought I knew what to look for, but..."

She held her hands out, empty palms up, then dropped them to her sides again.

"I wasn't calling for a progress report," Marta told her. "I needed to see how you're doing. That's all. I'm worried about how you're handling everything. And...I miss you."

If she wasn't going to make a discovery here, Sabine should at least have been by Marta's side.

Her stomach ached when she considered how many ways in which she was letting the other woman, and Heinrich, down. He'd have wanted her to look after his wife, wouldn't he?

"Hey, you might not have found the cure *yet*." Tosin's optimism bolstered her spirits a little. "But at least you got a boyfriend out of the deal."

"Oh, really?" Marta leaned closer to the screen, as if she could judge whether Miguel was worthy or not from those extra couple of inches.

Sabine didn't respond and instead glanced away at the lovely wooden deck and her bare toes, which curled against it.

"Ashamed of me, *lindeza*?" Miguel asked softly. He lifted her chin so she had no choice but to meet his piercing stare.

Could she keep making things worse? At least she seemed adept at that. Her fingers flew again to the necklace he'd given her, and she thought of the lost boy still buried deep within him. The one who'd been abandoned and never known how precious he was to those who loved him. "Of course not."

"It's okay to find happiness for yourself, Sabine," Marta assured her. "More than any scientific work, Heinrich would have been glad to see that."

What else was the woman going to say? That didn't make it okay.

Her affair with Miguel was irresponsible at best.

Sabine began to doubt herself. She wondered if she'd missed something because she'd been spending too much time with him instead of burning the midnight oil down here in the laboratory. Worse, maybe she'd screwed something up since some part of her didn't want to find the cure, because then she would have to leave.

Leave the *Divemaster*.

Leave her new friends.

Leave Miguel—the only man who'd ever made her wonder if she could do without him in a pathetically short amount of time.

In the background, Marta was still trying to reassure her, talking about enjoying her stay in Hawaii as much as possible, and how incredible the *Divemaster* had looked in the photos and stories she'd Googled.

"We'd love to have you onboard to see her for yourself sometime," Banks told Marta. Tosin and Miguel grinned simultaneously. They poked Banks out of the viewable range of the camera.

Sabine's eyes grew wide as she looked between Banks and her surrogate mother. It was nearly impossible to conceive of Marta with any man besides Heinrich. Except when she considered it objectively...they were about the same age. Both incredible people, who thrived on supporting those around them.

Maybe, someday, Marta would be ready to share her life with someone else.

A man like Banks would be an excellent choice, really.

And that felt like a betrayal.

Confused and hurting, Sabine couldn't take anymore.

Overwhelmed, she rasped, "Marta, I'm not feeling so good. It's been a long day, would you mind—"

"I'm going now. I just needed to hear your voice. To see you for myself. Let that boy take good care of you, understand?" Marta wagged her finger.

When had Sabine stopped being able to fend for herself? Her independent streak objected, strongly. She needed to be alone for a while. The *Divemaster* was enormous, but it was still a ship. There was nowhere to run. Nowhere to hide.

"I love you," Sabine whispered to Marta, terrified she might bawl if they didn't disconnect soon.

"I love you, too. Call me next time. When you're ready." With that, she was gone.

Staring at the blackened screen, Sabine didn't know which was worse—standing in front of Marta, facing deserved judgment that never came, or the absence of another important person from her life.

When Miguel put his hand on her shoulder and squeezed, she snapped. She shrugged out of his hold and pivoted on her heel, whipping around to face him.

Whatever unwise words were about to launch from her tongue froze when her timer went off.

She dashed to her workstation, scooped up her specimen, and slid it under the microscope.

If anything, the cancerous tissue appeared to be thriving instead of withering.

"Fuck!" She slapped her hands on the solid surface of the counter hard enough to make her wrists ache for days. In her peripheral vision, she saw Tosin and Banks slip from the lab, leaving her alone with Miguel. Probably for the best.

"You're even beautiful when you're throwing a tantrum," he said in an attempt to get her to laugh.

It didn't work.

"How long can we keep doing this?" She slashed a red marker through the latest on the list of eliminated specimens, then threw her notebook against the wall. "It's pointless!"

Sabine cringed as the pages fluttered then crumpled as it dropped to the ground.

"Are you objecting to the failed experiments or me fucking you so well every night that you hope you never find what you're looking for?" Miguel saw more than she gave him credit for sometimes.

"You arrogant bastard!" She wished she hadn't already chucked her pad or she would have flung it at his big head instead.

Instead of responding, he stalked closer, invading her space when all she wanted was to put some distance between them. She wasn't proud of herself, but she reached forward and shoved him, placing her palms flat against his chest as she leaned into the gesture.

Miguel didn't budge.

He smiled wolfishly then trapped her, his long fingers encircling her wrists. "Maybe. I've been holding out on you, though. Because you're twisting me up, too, *lindeza*. Enough is enough. I know what you need."

"To kick you in the balls?" She thrashed, not that it did her any good.

"You might want to watch that mouth of yours." He backed her against the wall then leaned in so all she could see was the compelling blue of his eyes. "It could get you in trouble tonight."

Why did his bullying turn her on? Despite his pseudo-threats, she was certain he was no risk to her. At least not to parts other than her heart, which seemed to forget more and more every day what her purpose onboard the *Divemaster* was supposed to be.

"Fuck this. I know what *we* need." Miguel didn't give her a chance to protest. He plucked her from the laboratory floor and tossed her over his shoulder as easily as if she was one of the tanks he hefted around day in and day out...not that she'd studied his form while he did it. "I have something to show you."

"Put me down." She shoved futilely at his back, her slaps utterly ineffectual.

The crack of his palm landing on her ass startled her more than the zing of sensation that raced from her cheek up her spine. She went dead still, wondering if he'd really just spanked her.

Before she could ask, or freak out, or surrender to the part of her that kind of liked it, he did it again. Then a third time.

"If you want to find out what's behind that black door in the middle of our hallway, you'll keep quiet and stop fighting me." Despite her instincts, which encouraged her to struggle, she went limp in his grasp. Admittedly, it felt better to rest on him than to try to break free.

Curiosity had always been both her biggest asset and her greatest downfall.

"Good girl," Miguel purred. "That's right. Let me make us both feel better."

NINE

Miguel had had enough. The past few days had gotten increasingly difficult, watching Sabine growing distant, smiling less. It had affected him in ways he wouldn't have imagined. After all, he was new at this—giving a shit about a partner's emotions and having responsibilities to her beyond providing a night chock full of orgasms.

Restlessness overtook him for the first time since they'd moved onboard the *Divemaster*. That urge he'd associated with wanderlust in the past—the compulsion that had prodded him to move on to the next place, and new people—maybe that sensation had been dissatisfaction all along. Or a certainty that he couldn't find what he was looking for there, so it was time to try somewhere else.

Except he no longer believed that picking up and moving would solve his problems or fill the void. No, after searching high and low, around the globe, the person who had the ability to quiet that restless part of him had found him instead. What a joke.

Sabine made him feel like Archer and Tosin made him feel. Waverly, too, for that matter. But stronger. Like he was taking his home with him, wherever he went, as long as they were near. Talking with Sabine was easy and entertaining. Sharing meals and work with her had the days flying by.

And the sex...son of a bitch. It was a miracle neither one of them had broken anything yet. Other than that one poor unfortunate chair he'd snapped a leg on when he'd bent her over it and gone a little wild. Shit, she made him feel so incredible he had hardly missed his extracurricular activities in the clubroom these past few weeks.

That was about to change.

He hoped he was making the right decision.

"Do you trust me, *lindeza*?" Miguel was as serious as he'd ever been in that moment. It wasn't a question he asked to boost his ego, or as some sort of foreplay. He had to know before he pushed her like this. Had to be certain he wouldn't frighten her away or do something that wasn't in her best interests.

Deep down, he knew she did. Hearing her breathe, "Yes," even as she hung upside from his rough hold had something in his gut unfurling, stretching, and getting ready to come out and play.

He'd never wanted to top a woman as badly as he did her.

That's why he needed help from someone impartial, who could call him off if he took things too far this first time. Especially after such a long vanilla stretch, who knew what would happen when he unleashed his darker side?

There were only two people he'd trust with that responsibility.

One of them happened to be up ahead, trying to ignore Miguel marching toward him in full caveman mode, Sabine tossed over his shoulder. Her lush ass filled his palm and she probably looked incredible with her wavy hair streaming down his legs. He peeked at their reflection in a window as he passed, shocked at the determination etched into his own features.

Why should he be, though? Their future hung in the balance, waiting to see how tonight turned out. He knew what he was praying for: that she responded to this part of him as well as she did the rest.

"Tosin, open the clubroom," he barked at his friend before Tosin could disappear into his own luxurious cabin.

"What?" The guy stopped mid-stride.

"You heard me." So had Sabine, if her renewed thrashing was any indication.

"Are you sure?" his friend asked. "There won't be any shutting that door again. For either of you, I think. Is this the right time for games?"

"Who's playing?" Miguel wondered. Not in a snarl or a roar, but in calm, collected tone that resonated with his conviction. Years of experience indulging his dominant side with ultra-willing women had taught him to trust his instincts. He knew what to do with Sabine.

Their problem was that he'd held back when he shouldn't have.

He'd let their budding relationship—because it wasn't some kind of experiment to him anymore—persuade him to change his ways. It wasn't going to work like that. And she was becoming too important to risk alienating by withholding part of himself from her.

Either she accepted all of him, fit as perfectly as he suspected she would, or there was no point in drawing out their eventual discord longer than necessary. They could have their fun, then go their separate ways.

A heaviness sank through his guts as if he'd swallowed the ship's main anchor.

Tosin took one look at his expression and nodded curtly. He strode ahead and entered the code only three people on the ship shared. Then he held the door wide, and admitted Miguel *and* Sabine.

"What—?" she gasped as she peeked around his waist. Even upside down there would be no mistaking the intent of the space. Heavy black leather furniture, maroon carpets and paint, and the massive selection of implements and BDSM equipment lit and exhibited like artwork made it pretty obvious how kinky the divemasters actually were.

Surprise.

How would Sabine take it?

"I figure it's a good sign that you're not trying to run away." Miguel lowered Sabine to the ground and slowly released her, hoping she didn't bolt.

She didn't.

Instead, she circumnavigated the clubroom, trailing her fingers along the nailheads on the edges of the bondage table before studying each of the assorted toys on display. He guessed she didn't have experience with them. In true Sabine style, she embraced her inquisitiveness.

"Well, I'm going to go ahead and assume you're not vampires since I've seen you sunning yourself mostly naked before," she said.

Tosin cracked up at that. "It does sort of have that vibe in here, doesn't it?"

"That doesn't mean we're not frightening to someone who doesn't understand what we like." Miguel swallowed hard. The last thing he wanted was to scare her.

"I'm always eager to learn." She turned to him then. "Are you going to teach me a lesson?"

Holy fuck.

She. Was. Perfect.

"Hell yes," he rasped as he practically charged her, scooping her into his arms. When he crushed his mouth to hers this time, he kissed her with everything he had, shielding her from nothing.

Instead of tensing, Sabine relaxed, allowing him to feast on her as he liked.

Why had he waited to bring her here? She was made for this.

For him.

When he feared she might pass out from lack of oxygen, he separated their mouths, giving her a temporary reprieve. Through ragged inhalations, she asked, "Why do we need a chaperone?"

Sabine peered over at Tosin, who'd made himself comfortable. The guy had already sunk into one of the giant wingback chairs, spread his legs wide, and slipped a hand inside the trunks he still wore after playing lifeguard on the ship's evening swim. The other glided over his bare chest as he watched Miguel introduce Sabine to their lifestyle as if it were the most enthralling movie he'd ever seen.

"Because, if you haven't noticed, I sort of lose my shit around you," he admitted. It was the least he could do given how vulnerable she might make herself to him tonight, if he was lucky. "Tosin is experienced. He'll have a clear mind and won't let anything happen to you."

"You're protecting me?"

"Of course," he answered immediately.

"I don't need that kind of insurance." She shook her head.

Maybe he did, though. Just this one time.

It didn't take a shrink analyzing him to figure out that he craved control because of the uncertainty of his childhood. This was how he'd survived. How he'd learned to conquer his insecurity and harness his fears. Turning those negatives into positive energy that had the power to elevate his lovers' experiences thrilled him over and over. With Sabine, though, the compulsion to imprint himself on her drove him to take her beyond the limits of his previous encounters.

Which could be a problem for her, especially during this introduction to power exchanges. It went against every coping mechanism she'd used herself. He tried harder to explain. "I know you've been on your own most of your life. You've had to be in charge and look out for yourself. Never let your guard down."

She peeked up at him then, daring him to deny she'd done a good job of it.

He wouldn't take that from her. No, he respected the strength it had required. But he could give her a break. Lift some of the burden off her shoulders. "Tonight, that's my job. I plan to do it very well. Focus every shred of my attention on that goal. The only thing you have to worry about is enjoying what I give you. Tosin will make sure we're both able to do that fully. Sound good?"

Sabine swallowed hard, then nodded. She asked, "Don't I need some kind of safe word?"

His brows raised. Maybe she wasn't as inexperienced as he'd thought.

"Hey, I read." She shrugged, making him chuckle.

"How about we keep it simple this time? Say stop, and I will. No questions asked. No hard feelings." He couldn't keep from touching her, running the backs of his knuckles over every bit of her exposed skin—her arms, her face, and especially the patch beside the necklace she'd inherited. It had always belonged there.

Banks had been dead right about that.

Sabine shivered, then nodded. Without being told, she pulled her sundress over her head and dropped it to the floor with a single seductive motion. A hissed curse came from Tosin's direction when her plump tits and curvy waist were unveiled. Only a scrap of lace remained, covering her pretty pussy.

Not for long.

⤳ TEN ⤶

"**I**'m going to choose the place," Miguel informed Sabine as he stalked toward her, closing the gap between them, however insignificant it was.

He pointed to a contraption they'd had specially made. It had been inspired by the hammocks they'd always had hanging around their bunkhouses, except this one had a far smaller chance of dumping someone out of it. Good thing, since a solid floor and not a sandy beach lay below it.

"You'll be bound to the sex net," he told her.

She didn't object.

"You're going to pick some toys you'd like me to use on you while I have you there." He grinned when she immediately looked toward the rack of nipple clamps. "See something you like?"

Sabine nodded.

"It does seem to make you come harder when I pinch them, or bite them." He nuzzled her bare breast, nipping the tip.

She shifted, rubbing her thighs together in response.

So he strode to the display and selected a pair that would make for a mild introduction.

"What else?" he asked, afraid to return to her side before collecting the rest of his gear. Otherwise, he might not find the willpower to abandon her again. He'd end up fucking her straight up, as he had the past several dozen times. At the end of the day, Sabine was enough for him, however she would take him.

She bit her lip.

"Can I make a suggestion?" Tosin asked her.

Sabine blinked a few times as if she'd forgotten he was there. Then she nodded, suddenly shy.

"Go for the rabbit fur flogger." He pointed to one of the instruments Miguel would have steered her to himself.

She nodded again. It thrilled Miguel that she trusted his friends nearly as much as she trusted him. That was critical if she was going to stay onboard after she'd finished her research.

Miguel drew up short, realizing he'd started to assume that she would. What if she didn't? What if she left to pursue her career or simply because—like he had so many times before—she felt it was time to move on?

It was too soon for promises. But he officially made it his goal to persuade her to stay from that moment forward. He wasn't ready to let her go and he doubted he would be any time soon.

He took his time plucking the tool from its holder so that he could school his expression. Tonight was about her. This moment they shared. Nothing more.

Before he could ask for another pick, she spoke up. "I liked what you did before."

Was that a blush spreading across her cheeks?

"You mean when I spanked you?" he clarified, though he already knew that's what she meant. Her pebbled nipples and parted lips didn't lie. Especially not when coupled with the slumberous gaze she shot him. He knew it well after the nights they'd spent together lately.

It had nothing to do with being sleepy and everything to do with being horny.

"Yes." She lifted her chin as if he'd think less of her for that. "I want something like that."

"Good girl." He smiled, knowing exactly the right thing. Within seconds, he had his favorite leather slapper in his hand along with the fur and the clamps. Quite an assortment.

Sabine was ready for this.

So was he.

Miguel strode to her, inspired when she didn't flinch from his rapid approach. Topping a woman as strong as her would be a highlight of his sexual experience. He set his implements on a small shelf on the post at the head of the fuck net. Then he spun to face Sabine.

He couldn't resist sampling her lips before lifting her, settling her onto the wide mesh made of silk ropes. He rocked her a bit, letting her get the feel for the motion of her new resting place. When she sighed, he pounced.

It only took him a few seconds to shackle her wrists to fur-lined cuffs. The restraints were attached to a bar fastened in the center to the post near her head. Then he did the same to her ankles, binding them to the matching bar on the pole by her feet. Spread wide before him, she was utterly at his mercy.

To prove it to them both, he bunched her panties in his fists.

"Not these, they're my favorite," she protested an instant before he ripped them from her as he had several other pairs lately. When would she learn it was better to go without around him?

"He'll buy you a dozen pair to replace them, sweetheart." Tosin laughed, though his humor was mixed with a solid dose of appreciation. From where he sat, he had a perfect view of her pussy. Could he see the arousal glistening between her legs?

Miguel bet he could.

Too bad he wouldn't get to smell it, or taste it, like Miguel would.

Though he'd like to drag out this encounter, making it last the whole night—or an entire lifetime, for that matter—he knew Sabine would only have so much in her this first time. Already her pulse fluttered and her cheeks burned with desire. It would wear her out to be left in suspense too long.

So he picked up the pace.

Miguel pinched open the nipple clamps. He loosened them slightly before setting them in place. Both at once. Then he let go gradually, increasing the pressure around her nipples until they decorated Sabine's spectacular tits better than a fistful of diamonds ever could.

She arched into the sensation, setting herself in motion again.

When the gentle swaying lulled her, Miguel moved forward. He took the flogger and dangled it above her, letting the falls dance over her in the barest of brushes. Along her collarbones and the upper swells of her breasts, he drew swirls that grew and grew until he covered most of her upper body.

He dipped toward her ribs, grinning wickedly when the soft flogger tickled her and she jerked.

"You can't escape, *lindeza*."

She whimpered. The sound stiffened his cock impossibly. Soon he would give in to the need for contact on his aching shaft. Once he did, he wouldn't be able to stop himself from fucking her madly. So he employed every scrap of patience he possessed.

When Sabine had relaxed, used to the sensual slide of the fur over her skin, he flicked his wrist just so. The ends whipped against her belly, making her yelp and twitch. The motion made the clamps on her breasts sway. Each reaction fed another and soon she was squirming, practically begging him to take her further.

So he did.

Miguel leaned down to kiss her and whisper praise in her ear. "You're doing so well, Sabine. You were made to be mine, weren't you?"

She hummed.

He thought so, too.

So he covered her with the second layer of the fuck net. She jerked as the ropes fell on her face and front. Before she could figure out what he was doing, he took hold of the rope sandwich she was the juicy meat of and flipped her over.

The rotating hardware did its job. Both the bars her arms and legs were attached to and the double layer of netting spun like a propeller. Now she lay face down instead of face up, her spectacular ass on display, bared for whatever he chose to do to it. A spanking tonight. Fucking some other time.

Miguel moved the unneeded top layer of the net out of the way for the moment.

He figured it was time to suit up. It wouldn't be long before the need to fuck her overwhelmed his good sense. Better to be prepared. But first...

His clothes hit the floor in record time, leaving him standing naked before Sabine and Tosin, too, though his friend was fixated on the gorgeous girl between them.

He took his cock in hand, wondering if it had ever been this painfully erect before in his life, and inched toward Sabine. He put one hand on her jaw and, using his thumb in the corner of her mouth, opened her lips so that he could guide himself inside the steaming paradise.

She sucked without having to be told, treating him to the variety of amazing tricks she'd mastered over the past several weeks. Having a repeat lover did have its benefits, he'd realized.

Miguel fisted his hands in her hair and held her still as he carefully thrust into her eager mouth.

When it was pull out or come down her throat, he retreated.

His teeth ground together as his body called him every sort of awful name it knew. It needed to come. In her. As soon as possible.

Tosin must have been able to tell he was wavering on the edge of his control. He held up a fancy glass dish that held a few dozen rubbers. "You want a condom?"

"Yes," Miguel answered at the same time that Sabine shouted, "No!"

"What's that?" he asked.

"I don't want you to wear one." She shook her head, about the only part of her she could move.

"I won't ever put you at risk." He held his hand out and caught the foil packet Tosin tossed him despite her protests. "Not in this or anything else."

"I'm saying stop to this. Please. You promised you would. It doesn't feel right in here." Some of her calm eroded as she struggled to find the words to convince him though lust slowed the functioning of her brain cells. "I'm on birth control. And clean. Tell me you are too and let's not put anything between us anymore."

He blinked. "You trust me that much?"

"I wouldn't have let you stick me to Spider-Man's porno web here if I didn't, would I?"

Tosin tried to disguise his bark of laughter.

Any other time, speaking to Miguel like that in the clubroom would earn her some extra swats with his slapper. Hell, it still might today. Except that deep down, he was glad. Overflowing with joy that she matched him here as well as elsewhere. He'd never been so relieved in his life.

Miguel cupped her cheek, letting his thumb caress her cheek in a gentle arc. "Okay, *lindeza*. If that's what you want, you're going to feel me in you. Bare. I'll fill you with my come. Sear you with my release. Show you just how much it turns me on to see you like this."

"Yes." She lifted her ass as best she could. "Fuck me. Please."

"Aren't you forgetting something?" He took the slapper from the shelf and let her feel the cool leather on her ass for just a moment before he gave her the first swat.

If it had slipped her mind, she remembered now.

Sabine gasped. Then her ass rose again. So he repeated the gesture.

He wasn't counting his strokes, didn't need to because he could clearly sense the shift in her. At first, she indulged him, playing a sexy game that turned her on too, if the increasing sweetness of her scent told the truth.

She quickly moved beyond that stage and settled in, letting the repeated stinging blossom into something more meaningful than a mere form of entertainment, or a cheap thrill. The moment he'd put her over his shoulder in the laboratory, he knew this was what she needed.

No longer was he going to let her keep her most intense reactions bottled inside.

If venting was what she needed, he'd provide a safe outlet. One that would allow her to manage her stress. In a safe environment, he'd help her drain the poison from her system and replace it with rapture. A few more strokes and she'd be there.

A sniffle came from her.

Though his palms ached to rub her ass, soothe the inflammation, he knew that's not what *she* needed. But Sabine was stubborn and he wasn't sure she was ready for the pain it might take to set her free.

One more. And then another.

A sob escaped Sabine. Never once did she ask him to stop and he was reluctant to insult her by doing so now.

"Miguel," Tosin warned.

"Not yet," he replied. "She's nearly there."

"Or it's almost too much." His friend spoke up, addressing Sabine directly. "Isn't it?"

She didn't respond, lost in her own headspace.

Miguel took his friend's advice into consideration. It was, after all, why he'd given the man a front row seat to this show, the most important scene of Miguel's life so far.

His fingers shook as they cupped Sabine's chin, tilting her face toward him while he leaned down so that he could study her glassy eyes from a fraction of an inch away. The fire he saw, still banked deep within them, along with unbearable agony gave him the courage to take them both where he knew they needed to go.

She had to let the sadness and anger bleed from her soul so that she could channel her energy into something productive again.

He could perform that operation for her.

Sabine hovered right there, on the edge of breaking. He had the skill and the power to take her where she needed to go without pushing too hard. He hoped.

"One more." Miguel nuzzled her temple before placing a tender kiss there. "Let go, Sabine. Give me everything inside you. I can handle it."

He brought the slapper down again, hard, at the base of her cheeks.

The shockwave of pain seemed to rip through her this time. She cried out.

Huge, heaving sobs worked through her.

Miguel dropped the slapper on the floor. He tugged the top net down, flipped her again, then straddled the fuck net, which flexed to accommodate his stance. The contraption could easily hold both of their full weights. Face to face, he wrapped her in his heat and put as much of his skin as he could into contact with hers. He was sure she hadn't let herself exorcise these demons since Heinrich had died. Maybe not even since her parents had been forced to leave her behind.

Right then he promised himself he wouldn't abandon her.

Not ever.

If she walked first, that would be one thing. But he'd never let her go if he didn't have to.

As he soothed her, her shudders began to transform. It took a while, but eventually she was calling out, ready for him to soothe her in another, more primal, fashion. "Miguel?"

"I'm here, *lindeza*."

"I need—"

"My cock?"

"You!" she cried in response. "I need *you*."

He wondered if the subtle difference in her phrasing had been intentional. Either way, he wasn't about to deny her. He couldn't bear to be outside her a single moment longer.

Miguel nodded. "In that case..."

Without further hesitation he took himself in hand and aimed the head of his cock between her legs, then drilled forward. The shock of being so empty and then suddenly so full—filled with him—seemed to steal Sabine's breath.

It was like their lives.

One moment they'd been alone.

And then they'd met.

Ever since, it'd been like this. Complete, bursting with passion and laughter and pleasure. Even during some of the darkest times she'd experienced. That she could open herself to him, allow him to connect with her despite the darkness, made him work harder to deserve her affection.

That was a gift he never would have been bold enough to ask for. Or even to dare wish for.

Miguel began to move, withdrawing completely before plunging balls-deep within her.

Sabine's gaze winged from his face to Tosin's hand, which flew along the length of his cock as he perched on his seat as if it were a throne and he a king watching his servants perform for his delight. Then she'd glance back at the intersection of their bodies. She was so busy observing that she had started to lift out of the trance-like state he'd worked so hard to put her in.

That would not do. It was more important for her to feel and be honest with herself about her emotions in the moment. Yet he couldn't bring himself to stop fucking her long enough to fix the problem.

"Tosin," he grunted.

"Yeah?" His friend seemed startled when addressed. His steady jerking hitched.

"Blindfold my beautiful pet."

She shook her head violently, so he put his hand carefully around her neck, keeping her still. All the while he drove into her, addicted to the feel of her body trying to pull him in farther. When she could, she explained, "I like to see you. Him."

"Not this time," Miguel refused, knowing better than her what she needed at the moment. "Feel instead. Feel me. More important, feel what's coming from within you. Go ahead, close your eyes."

She did.

Tosin was there to wrap a scrap of black silk around her face to keep her from disobeying even as the ecstasy he gave her mounted. Her pussy began to hug him tighter, sucking him deeper into her body.

"*Lindeza*, you've never been more stunning to me than you are right now," he promised as he plowed into her, his feet still planted on the ground giving him enough leverage to shake the fuck net violently. Hell, their exchange felt momentous enough to rock the entire ship. "The only thing that will make you more gorgeous is your release. I can't wait to see you come for me. On me."

"Miguel!" she screamed. "Please!"

As he'd expected, the lack of sight had turned her concentration inward, magnifying her own feelings.

"That's so good." He couldn't wait to reward her. "Go ahead. Come for me."

Sabine threatened to smother his cock in velvety warmth. Her body simultaneously drew him in and nearly squeezed him out. Oh no, he wasn't going anywhere.

Miguel fucked deeper. Harder.

He embedded himself as far inside her as he could get while she quaked and came.

And when she relaxed the slightest bit, he pumped into her mercilessly, only then freeing his restraint on his own pent up desire. His balls drew tight to his body and he swore he shot so hard he might have broken something.

As he pumped jet after jet of come into her depths, she cried out again, her climax rejuvenating as he flooded her pussy.

Far in the background of his awareness, he heard Tosin finding his own relief.

How could he watch Sabine unravel like that and not be affected?

Miguel didn't blame his friend in the least.

For a while, he added his weight to the fuck net, sprawled on top of Sabine, crushing her at least a little. She didn't seem to mind though, as she moaned softly on occasion. Her pussy massaged him with periodic aftershocks that extended their bliss. A particularly strong one rolled through her when he unfastened the clamps on her breasts before sucking each nipple lightly, soothing it.

When he could manage to lift his head, he kissed her as gently and sweetly as he knew how.

She deserved his reverence.

Tranquil in the aftermath of their tempestuous emotions and the outlet he'd provided, it jolted him when she gasped a few minutes later.

"Miguel!" she shrieked. "Miguel, it's like I'm blind!"

"It's only silk, *lindeza*." He shushed her with feather-light kisses as he worked quickly to untie the knot. While he did that, Tosin rushed to her and unfastened her restraints, freeing her almost instantly. "You're fine, I promise. I'm right here."

"I know." She stilled then. "I'm not afraid."

"Then what's wrong?" he wondered as he slipped the blindfold over her hair, marveling at the contrast of her nearly platinum waves against the midnight silk. Other women might consider it unruly or in need of a cut. He liked that she left it natural, untamed, and slightly uneven. When the wind blew through it on deck, she reminded him of a cross between a gypsy sailor and a super sexy pirate. Especially when he took in the sea glass necklace of his, wrapped around her throat.

"The darkness." She blinked furiously as she returned to her senses. She tried to sit up, so he helped her into position, hanging onto her so she couldn't tumble out of the net while he looked to Tosin for help. Had his orgasm addled his brains or was she not making any sense?

His friend only shrugged.

"It's the darkness, Miguel. It blinds you." Sabine squirmed until he lifted her and set her on her feet. She began to pace, freaking him out just a little. He'd unlocked something within her. It was his job as a dominant to help her work through it, but he'd never seen something like this before.

Didn't know how to support her other than to assure her he would take care of her and give her anything she needed. "We don't have to do that again, *lindeza*. I'm sorry if I upset you."

Had he judged everything wrong?

"No! It was perfect. Exactly right." She waved her hands at him, making her breasts bounce as she turned to him with the most brilliant smile he'd ever seen. "Don't you understand?"

"Not a clue here, honey," Tosin answered for him as he cleaned up the massive load he'd shot across his chest and abs. "Can you break it down for us non-geniuses in the room?"

"Heinrich said we had to blind ourselves or we might never look at the answer in a way that allowed us to see it." She practically buzzed with excitement.

"So you think…" He started to see where she was coming from.

"We're going night diving, Miguel." Sabine's enormous smile dazzled him with its brilliance.

"I'll get the UV torches and see how much bottom time Archer has left today." Tosin already headed for the door.

"You should probably put some clothes on!" Miguel shouted after him. "Safety first—wouldn't want an eel to bite that thing off, would you?"

Tosin jogged back into the clubroom and hopped into his trunks. "Good looking out, man."

"That's what friends are for." He clapped Tosin on the back, hoping the other man knew how grateful he was for his participation that evening. If nothing else, he'd have someone to relive the night with, someone who could vouch for the intensity of the experience when he began to doubt it could have been as incredible as he remembered.

If Sabine left him, at least he'd have that memory. Forever.

"Anytime," Tosin muttered, too quietly for Sabine to hear. "No, seriously. *Anytime*. Lucky bastard."

ELEVEN

S abine's heart raced as they skimmed the moonlit waves toward the silhouette of Molokini. Other than the whir of the outboard engine on the rigid hull inflatable tender and the slap of waves against its side, there were no sounds. Even the army of nesting seabirds that made the scrap of land their sanctuary had hunkered down for the night.

"Are you sure you're up for this?" Miguel asked. "You've already had a crazy day. Going under at night can be challenging, especially if you've never done it before."

Honestly, she was scared shitless.

But if she had trusted the man to take her on the intimate journey he had earlier, holding her life in his hands wasn't much more of a stretch. The things he'd done to her—not the physical ones, but the emotional ones—caused her to shiver despite the balmy overnight temperature.

Miguel drew her closer to his side and rubbed her arm, transfusing his heat and confidence into her. The three men onboard looked between each other, silently communicating.

"Tosin and I are more than happy to do this dive for you," Archer offered. "You two can chill up here and man the boat while we collect samples. Tomorrow night, when you're better prepared, we can dive in two teams."

"No, no." Sabine waved them off despite the temptation. Following in Heinrich's footsteps, or flipper kicks, had become an obsession. She had to see this through.

They slowed as they approached a mooring ball and Tosin began to tie the boat off.

"If at any time you want to call the dive, just give me the thumbs-up signal and we'll make a controlled ascent immediately," Miguel promised. "I know this area super well now. I promise you I can get us back to the boat from anywhere within the crater."

"Which site are we at?" She tried to orient herself against the islet. Everything looked different at night. Further apart.

"This is Middle Reef," Tosin told her. "It bottoms out between fifty and sixty feet, so you don't have to worry about dropping too far or narcing yourself by accident. Not that Miguel would let that happen even if you could."

Sabine nodded. Nitrogen narcosis referred to disorientation suffered by divers breathing certain gases at high pressure. In less than ninety feet of water, the risk decreased drastically. The chemistry of the phenomenon fascinated her. That didn't mean she felt the need to experience it herself. Although it was easy to cure by rising until the pressure decreased and symptoms abated, once in an altered state of consciousness—confused and numb—it could be difficult to remember how to react properly.

Many unfortunate sufferers had mistaken up for down and only made the situation worse, or drifted off until they ran out of air. In the inky darkness below, it would be even more difficult to know which direction the surface was if you weren't alert enough to monitor your own bubbles for clues.

She shivered.

"If we sit around talking long enough, I'm going to chicken out." She clipped her buoyancy control vest into place and fastened the cummerbund so that her tanks were secure, then double-checked her fins and pulled on her mask.

"Don't do something you're not comfortable with." Miguel gave her one last out.

"Sometimes pushing your limits can be terrifying. It's also extraordinarily rewarding." She took his hand then, hoping he realized she'd enjoyed the hell out of the rush he'd given her earlier and wanted to go two for two tonight. "I need to do this."

"Then I'm with you. And I'm not letting go." He kept his word, holding her fingers tight as Archer and Tosin helped them get situated on the rounded sidewall of the tender. Tosin flicked on a torch that she would swear could be seen from space considering how It sliced through the darkness. He also pressed a plastic bubble on her tank, which began to glow so Miguel could spot her if they were separated, she guessed.

Thinking about that possibility didn't alleviate her anxiety any.

"I had an idea," Miguel said to her, just before they were set to go. "You know how Heinrich's message to you said we needed to look at things differently?"

She nodded.

"We sometimes dive with UV lights instead of these super bright full spectrum ones. It allows you to detect the florescence in coral polyps. It's really awesome-looking, but I never thought about the fact that it might let you see different things than you would with the standard torch," he explained.

"Can you see well enough to collect samples with the UV light?" she wondered.

"Definitely."

"Then let's try it." She held her lamp out to Tosin and he exchanged it for one of the UV variety. Miguel's too. "If nothing else, it'll be pretty, right?"

"Nowhere near as beautiful as you, *lindeza*." Miguel snuck in a quick kiss then put his regulator in his mouth. She followed his lead.

On his count of three, they did a backward roll. Tumbling through the water, she panicked. Her breaths came in and out faster, filling her vision with a riot of bubbles.

Miguel's firm squeeze on her fingers reminded her that she wasn't alone.

She calmed her respiration and opened her eyes, which had been squeezed shut.

Staring at her from less than a foot away, Miguel used his thumb and forefinger to make a circle while his other three fingers were extended. The universal signal for okay.

She flashed it back.

With him, she was.

He nodded then changed his gesture to a thumbs-down, indicating they should begin their descent. As she lay flat and aimed the ultraviolet beam of her light toward the reef, she gasped.

It wasn't dark or eerie as she had expected. The sea floor teemed with life. Typical daytime fish were nowhere to be seen, hiding from nocturnal predators while they rested. In their place, a cluster of ctenophores—some sort of comb jelly, she thought—drifted by like a fleet of mini UFOs. Lights twinkled from inside the organisms as they propelled themselves through the currents.

The hard corals she'd spent so much time staring at the past few weeks had also been altered. Instead of their calcium carbonate skeletons, which were typically the only visible part of the animal, the polyps themselves had emerged and the coral heads were unrecognizable. Animated, instead of rocklike. Their tentacles swayed in the surge and waved around as they caught zooplankton that drifted past. Neon colors reflected by the UV rippled in a mesmerizing light show caused by the undulating motion.

It was like visiting the same reef in an alternate universe. How had she never done this before?

They closed in on a mound of cauliflower coral. While Miguel carefully took a sample, she peered around, transfixed by their surroundings. Though she'd seen pictures of these phenomena before, witnessing it firsthand was something else entirely.

Sabine turned to Miguel, her eyes wide. He flashed her the okay hand signal, a question.

She nodded vigorously.

With his fingers and palm now flat in a blade, he held his arm out straight, indicating the direction to swim for their next collection. Again, she wanted to kick herself for taking time to enjoy the view before getting down to business. How could you not be awed by this scenery, though?

They worked as efficiently as possible. Given the other dives they'd done that day, they couldn't afford to stay down at sixty feet more than thirty minutes without requiring a decompression stop. The time flew by as quickly. Too soon, they were preparing to ascend.

Not before she'd spotted an octopus hunting and took a few moments to admire a free-swimming Javanese eel that was even longer than Miguel. With a reluctant sigh, she took one final look around.

Which was when she thought she saw the flicker of a white beam of light, brighter than the UV variety she and Miguel carried. She shook the metal cylinder hanging from her BC to get her divemaster's attention. He whipped his head around. But when she tried to point to what she'd seen, it had vanished.

She shrugged and shook her head.

Maybe it had only been the shimmering of another of these wondrous night dwellers.

Miguel tapped his dive computer, reminding her of their deadline, then ascended slowly along the mooring line she hadn't even noticed until they were within an arm's length of the cord. They went up it until they hovered fifteen feet below the surface. After a ninety-second safety stop, they were back on the surface.

Archer and Tosin reached down to lift her into the boat.

Due to the nitrogen load they'd taken on during their regular daily dives, they had even less bottom time available. Especially since they were picking up Miguel's divemaster slack, though they'd never once complained.

"What'd you see down there?" Miguel asked when he'd joined her in the boat.

"I'm not sure. Maybe just a funny reflection. For a second, I thought it was another dive light. A white one. But since the guys are already up here, I guess it wasn't that." She shrugged as she began to break down her gear while Archer got them underway, returning to the *Divemaster* with some more work for her to do.

"We used UV lights, too," Tosin said. "Not full spectrum."

The guys exchanged another one of those infamous stares, probably saying she was clearly nuts, so she changed the subject. "How many samples did we get? I hope I can process them all before tomorrow night so we know what to concentrate on next...if we don't already have the winner."

She grinned at that. They had to be closing in on Heinrich's secret.

"*Lindeza*, you need to sleep first." Miguel didn't seem like he was going to listen to her arguments about how she could power through with the help of a gallon or so of black coffee. It might be hard for him to take her seriously when a huge yawn escaped her at the reminder.

Even harder would have been for her to persuade him in any fashion when she was unconscious, which she was by the time they arrived back at the ship. The ups and downs of the day had sapped her energy.

It was a good thing she rested before tackling her next round of experiments, because none of them panned out. On the bright side, she got to experience the gorgeous nightly display over and over with Miguel by her side. It never grew old, though she had to keep reminding herself that it would be better if they had achieved their goal even if it meant the end of her quality time with her favorite divemaster.

Nearly two weeks after her first night dive, Sabine stumbled from her laboratory and plopped onto the dive platform, dangling her legs behind the *Divemaster* as she watched the waves roll by endlessly.

Her renewed optimism had suffered the same fate as her original bout of worthless enthusiasm following more than a dozen fruitless collecting expeditions. Everyone was feeling the strain of their pointless trips.

They'd all agreed to take a night off and regroup.

A month into her research, she wasn't a single step closer to figuring out exactly what Heinrich had uncovered. If she didn't stumble across it soon, she'd have to admit it wasn't here to find. Then pick a different approach. She'd already inconvenienced Archer, Tosin, and *especially* Miguel long enough.

It would be nearly impossible to find someone who'd fund continuing research with this mammoth failure under her belt, even if she could figure out where to look next. Maybe another Indo-Pacific location that had been on Heinrich's route. Hell, she might have to return to Germany to regroup. Sabine would see if she could salvage anything from Heinrich's home computer or the rubble of his laboratory.

The odds of that tactic being productive were even worse than those of the Molokini Crater divulging its secrets to her at this point.

Worse, it would mean saying goodbye to Miguel.

How many blows could she take before they crushed her?

∽ TWELVE ∾

Miguel finished tucking the last of the items for their excursion into his backpack and zipped it as quietly as possible. Sabine needed every minute of rest she could stockpile. The experiment, and the lack of results she desperately hoped for, weighed on her more and more.

When he'd fallen asleep with her in his arms the night before, he'd noticed her hipbones dug into him a bit. Using gentle caresses, he surveyed the rest of her and was convinced she'd gotten thinner during her stay. Consistently shorting herself on sleep had given her dark circles below her eyes that hadn't been there before, either.

This time he knew better than to let her reach her breaking point. She needed to step away for a quick break so she could stay positive. Clarity of mind was a job requirement she couldn't meet when she got too down on herself. Not even their clubroom sessions seemed to help her relax as much as they had at first.

Maybe because the more attached they grew to each other, the more troubling it was to consider what would happen if she didn't make progress soon.

Miguel had considered that as he beat the stuffing out of the punching bag in the ship's gym during his past few workouts. He had the bruised knuckles to show for it, too.

Fortunately, he had an idea about how to help her rejuvenate. One that involved less intensity and, hopefully, more fun than his previous methods. That's not to say they hadn't been enjoying some quality time in the clubroom. Because—oh, fuck—had they. Even there, she was his well-balanced counterpart.

It was just that he felt compelled to show her that great sex wasn't the *only* thing he cared about because he might have to make his case soon for why she shouldn't leave him. What if he couldn't persuade her to stay when the time came?

In the back of his mind, he thought about the out Archer had given him. One he'd never planned to take. Could he sell his share of the *Divemaster*? Would he if that was what it took to follow Sabine wherever she needed to go next?

Incredibly, he was starting to consider the possibility.

With everything ready, he couldn't delay waking her any longer. If he did, they'd miss the main event. Stalking to the side of the bed, he took a few precious moments to memorize what she looked like as she slept in his bed. Facedown, sprawled across most of the wide-open space, she'd burrowed into the super soft sheets wearing nothing but his necklace, which she'd never once taken off. Though she'd only found her place there a month ago and could be a total cover hog, he couldn't imagine what it would be like to climb into bed alone after sharing it with her.

He wouldn't.

If she wasn't there, he didn't want to be either.

Whoa.

Miguel drew a deep breath then knelt beside the bed. He shook her shoulder lightly, awed as always by the softness of her skin. "Good morning, *lindeza.*"

He waited for her to smile at him slowly before he placed a kiss on her cheek.

"Am I late for the lab?" She closed her eyes for a moment as if psyching herself up, then pushed onto her elbows. He tried not to stare at her rack, or even to notice how amazing it was, in case he fell back into bed with her to wake her up properly. They didn't have time for that.

"Not exactly." He handed her a bra and underwear—practically a crime—along with a soft T-shirt and a pair of comfortable shorts. "Get dressed."

"Is something wrong?" She bit her lower lip.

Miguel hated that disaster came to her mind as the first motivation for his actions. "Nope. Everything's great. It's a field day. Or I guess, if you want to be more grown up about it, I'm taking you out on a date."

"Huh? You are?" She pushed fully upright, rubbed the last lingering bit of sleep from her eyes with her fists, then perked up, always down for an adventure.

Could she be any more adorable?

"Yep." He stole one more kiss then tweaked her nipple. "Hurry up. We don't want to miss our ride."

"Where are we going?" she wondered.

"You'll have to come with me to find out." He nudged her toward the edge of the mattress.

Sabine took the clothes, hopped from bed, and scampered to the bathroom still naked, giving him a great view of her ultra-spankable ass and long legs.

Damn, maybe he should have woken her up just a little earlier. He rubbed the growing bulge in his cargo shorts.

She'd taken care of business, brushed her teeth, and reappeared in a few minutes, fully dressed. He liked that about her. Sabine didn't bother wasting time primping, didn't need to because she was so damn gorgeous naturally.

He already had his backpack over his shoulder.

"Let's go!" She darted ahead of him out the door and down the hall. Her easy smiles and genuine enthusiasm made his hours of planning worth it.

"Up to the helipad," he told her when they neared the elevator.

"Ohh, fun." She clapped then poked the button for the appropriate deck.

Miguel couldn't help but laugh. He drew her to him and squeezed her tight. "It's so great to see you happy again."

She froze. Had he said exactly the wrong thing?

"Maybe we shouldn't go." She swallowed hard enough that he heard it. "The samples—"

"Can wait one day." He'd prepared this argument. "You need time off, a mini vacation, and when we get back you'll be twice as effective, making up any delay."

Miguel expected her to argue. She didn't.

She must have felt even worse than he'd realized. Shit.

The elevator dinged and opened onto the deck with the helipad. Waverly and the chopper stood by. He kissed Sabine's forehead then swung his backpack around so he wore it on his chest. She looked at him funny until he turned and crouched. "Piggyback ride?"

Whatever he could do to keep her smiling today, he would gladly do it.

"Woot!" She hopped on, wrapping her legs around him. The heat of her core against him had a million other dirty thoughts racing through his mind. She hugged his shoulders and laid her cheek against one of them.

As he jogged, he heard her say softly, "Thank you, Miguel."

"You can thank me properly later," he said with a wink as he reached the chopper and helped her inside.

"Noted." She blew him a kiss, then glanced around as if only now realizing it was still dark out. "I think I'm jacked up from our night dives. What time is it?"

"Four fucking thirty in the morning," Waverly grumbled. "Who takes someone on a date at the ass crack of dawn?"

Miguel laughed. "Sorry, babe. Tell Banks to give you a bonus for putting up with outlandish requests."

"It's not the request that's a pain, it's the owner," she mock-grumbled even as she smiled. "Happy to take you anywhere, anytime, you know that. Now hop in and let's get going."

He kissed her cheek then climbed inside, taking a seat next to Sabine on the triple-wide bench side of the passenger area across from two captain chairs that were extremely comfortable but far too separate from each other. The center seat had been folded down to make a table and an assortment of fruit, juices, croissants, and yogurt was laid out.

Sabine was digging in. This had definitely been a good idea.

He owed the kitchen staff a personal thanks when they returned, too. On the floor, he spotted another delivery from them that he'd need later. Perfect.

When they'd buckled in, Waverly lifted off so smoothly they didn't even have to hang on to their glasses. She had mad skills.

Licking pineapple juice from her fingers, Sabine peeked out the window. Miguel did the same. The view from up here never ceased to impress. He remembered when he'd first met their resident scientist. Could it really have only been a month ago? They'd made this trip in reverse and she'd asked about the Haleakala Observatory.

"Are we going to see the sunrise from the summit of Haleakala?" She practically bounced in her seat as she swung around to face him. "It's supposed to be amazing. Did you know Haleakala actually means 'House of the Sun'?"

"I didn't, no."

"Sorry, is my inner nerd showing?" She grimaced as she brushed her hair out of her eyes.

"Just a little." He finished the job for her then leaned in for a quick kiss. "No worries, I think she's cute."

More like Miguel loved this side of her. He wondered if he could convince her to wear thick-rimmed glasses and a plaid skirt for him in bed sometime.

He grinned as she rattled off facts to him and Waverly without stopping to draw a breath. "The summit is 10,023 feet above sea level. There's a plant you can find around the main parking area called a silversword that's endangered. People walk right by it and don't even realize how rare it is. The observatory on top of the mountain is run by the University of Hawaii Institute for Astronomy and it's regarded as one of the best in the world in part because it sits above the tropical inversion layer, so the view is crystal clear from there."

He had no idea what that meant, but he nodded anyway, feeling better and better about his itinerary for the day. They landed a few minutes later. He helped Sabine into the foul-weather jacket he'd brought for her, handed her the shoes she'd had to give up when onboard the *Divemaster*, then snagged the two-man sleeping bag he'd stowed along with the rest of his supplies.

Sabine asked Waverly if she wanted to join them for the sunrise. She declined, opting to stay with her helicopter instead.

Silently, Miguel thanked her. Not that he didn't love the woman, in a completely platonic sort of way, but he felt some indescribable urge to have Sabine to himself today. They spent so much time around others onboard the *Divemaster* that it was a rare treat.

He figured that was one reason his relationship with Sabine seemed so intense. They'd been together damn near every second of the past month. And yet he wanted more.

On a relatively level spot, he laid out the sleeping bag and a thermos of Sabine's favorite hot tea then climbed in beside her, drawing her onto his lap. She cuddled up to him, curling into his embrace.

For a while, they sat there in silence, observing the stars.

She was right—they did look unbelievable from up here. If he lifted his hand, he might be able to pluck one from the sky for her. Gradually, the dots were joined by hints of color that illuminated the clouds, which were actually below his and Sabine's perch. The sky looked like the ocean on calm mornings when fog blanketed the surface.

Golden rays gilded the wisps, which began to be offset by a background of salmon and burnt oranges. Finally, the sun peeked above the horizon, setting the vibrant colors to shame. And when the magic faded, leaving behind a bright, beautiful day, Sabine cheered.

He caught her as she turned to him and kissed her, savoring the flavor of tropical fruit mingled with her lips.

Miguel made love to her mouth as thoroughly as a public park would permit. The entire time, he stared into her eyes, which gazed right back at him, never shying away from the bond that shone brighter than that epic sunrise had.

"I think I'm ready to go home now," she whispered.

It thrilled him that she had called the *Divemaster* home. Nearly as much as it affected him to realize she was equally eager to get him in bed as he was to have her there.

"Are you sure?" He kissed the tip of her nose. "Because it turns out I know people who fund a shit-ton of grants. Including ones to the Institute of Astronomy."

As of two days ago, anyway. *Thank you, Banks.*

Sabine's eyes went wide. "Seriously?"

"Yup." He nodded. "Out of respect for their patrons, they've arranged for us to take a quick peek around the facilities. You know, unless you would rather split. I'm not opposed to taking you back to bed if you prefer."

Well, okay, it wasn't an either or proposition. He'd do that later. There was no way she'd pass up this chance.

Sabine squirmed from the sleeping bag and yanked on his hand. "Come on!"

He didn't release her fingers during the trek to the observatory or the admittedly interesting tour they were taken on by one of the leading researchers. Sabine asked tons of technical questions, but Miguel zoned out, spending his time wondering about what might be out there in space and if he could ever find a place, a home, a group of friends, and a lover that made him as content as he was at the moment.

When he decided the answer was a resounding no, he knew it was official.

He'd fallen for Sabine.

Lost in thought, he almost didn't hear the latest man they were being introduced to ask Sabine about Heinrich. The slight uptick in her tone and the way she stepped closer to Miguel alerted him to the situation.

He put his arm around her waist, cursing the probably well-meaning fuckface for reminding her of things Miguel couldn't fix for her, not even with the influence of several billion of Archer's dollars.

"So what are you doing in the area?" Professor Bookworm asked her. "Working on a new project? Or maybe something of his he hadn't finished before he passed away?"

The question seemed a little too casual and way too insensitive for Miguel's liking. "Sorry, I didn't catch your name. Who are you again?"

The guy shrugged. "I'm Brad Post. Just a grad assistant around here."

"It's been nice talking to you, Brad. But if you'll excuse us, we've got somewhere else to be." Yeah, like anywhere people weren't asking too many questions about something Heinrich had been trying to keep under wraps or topics that hurt his woman to discuss.

Sabine nodded. "Thank you for the tour, Dr. Pickering."

They exchanged handshakes before Miguel and Sabine retraced their steps to the helicopter.

"You okay?" he asked Sabine.

"Fine." She smiled, though some of the shine had dulled. "Lots of people know he was my mentor. Especially in academic circles—everyone knows everyone."

"Then you're up for more fun?" He could salvage the rest of the day, he figured.

"I'm not sure how you can top this." She rose onto her tiptoes and kissed him sweetly. "Honestly, Miguel. This is the nicest thing someone's ever done for me. You know, other than the whole *Divemaster* thing. But this is...personal."

"Yeah, it damn well is." He kissed her this time, lingering for a while. Their next activity wouldn't be very comfortable with a boner, though, so he reined himself in before he could get carried away.

"So what now?" Resilient and tough as ever, Sabine perked up again.

He strode to the cargo hold of the helicopter and withdrew two bikes along with helmets and other protective gear.

Waverly met them around back and held out the picnic basket he'd spotted earlier. "Are you going to be able to balance that on your handlebars?"

He laughed. "Don't insult me. Of course. I can even ride with no hands."

Sabine shook her head. "Have you ever seen what the road down from here looks like? It's no joke. Hands the whole way, please. I need you in one piece for the things I have planned for tonight."

"I like the sound of that." He gave in to the disapproving stares of two kickass women. "I bet I can fit this stuff in my backpack. Will that make you feel better?

"Yes," they answered together.

So he stuffed as much as possible in there then hefted it onto his shoulders.

"I'm going to fly down to the Kula Botanical Garden. They've got a spot for me to land. Take your time and call me if your plans change." Waverly hugged Sabine then waved. "Be careful!"

"It's been a while since I've actually ridden a bike." Sabine made a funny face as she climbed on.

"The good news is it's entirely downhill. All you have to do is glide." He watched her as she took off in front of him, mentally rating this portion of the day with five solid gold stars when he realized her ass would be on display for him to perv over the whole way down the mountain. That was more likely than a picnic basket to make him wreck.

She may not have had a lot of practice, but in customary Sabine style, that didn't keep her from going for it whole-heartedly. He loved that about her. Always willing to try new things, or check something out, she never shied away from new experiences.

He hoped they could have lots of those together.

Wind stung his cheeks as they picked up speed.

Sabine proved to be quite the daredevil, taking the hairpin switchbacks in the mountain road far faster than he was comfortable with. It was a long way down on the other side of the guardrails, when there were guardrails. Maybe he shouldn't have unleashed her.

Watching her hair whip around her and hearing her exclamations float over the stark beauty of the cinder desert surrounding them, he fed off of her elation.

Together they whooped and hollered to each other, pointing out highlights as they wormed their way toward the park where Waverly waited with their ride home. Lush tropical trees and flowers soon replaced the barren landscape of the summit.

Another of Hawaii's many ecosystems engulfed them in greens so vivid they made him think of the variety of blues that made up the ocean. Underwater would always be his favorite place, the pinnacle of nature to him. This wasn't too shabby, though.

When they coasted into the parking lot at the botanical garden, Sabine turned toward him—face flushed, eyes bright. He helped her climb off her bike and steady herself before leading her along a path to the spot he'd picked for lunch.

A half-mile down the trail, he heard the rush of water. A few more turns through the jungle and an enormous waterfall loomed above them. Moss clung to the rocks on either side of the long, ribbony stream, which poured over the edge of the cliff hundreds of feet in the air.

"It's gorgeous." Sabine paused, staring up at the feature in awe.

"I *still* haven't seen anything that comes close to you, *lindeza*. Never will." Miguel took her in his arms, simply hugging her tight. He buried his nose in her hair and breathed deep of the scent of clean mountain air blended with her.

While she wandered around the clearing snapping photos, including a bunch of selfies of them laughing and goofing off together, he spread out their blanket and unpacked the gourmet feast. For the first time since they'd met, they enjoyed normal people stuff together.

Okay, normal people stuff, if you were extraordinarily lucky and privileged, too.

He refused to feel guilty about the perks he could provide his companion after working hard and building his life from nothing. Because he knew that even if he was still dirt poor, it wouldn't matter.

They only needed each other.

Sabine smiled up at him. Her fingers played with his hands. Stuffed, and in need of a power nap, he grinned back. "You ready to head home?"

"Will that lead to your dick in my pussy sometime soon?" She surprised him with her directness, as always.

He laughed. "Definitely."

"After the best blowjob of your life, of course, for being such an amazing—" She hesitated, as if unsure of what to call him, until finishing with, "lover."

Except it sounded like more of a question by the time she got to the end of her sentence.

He wondered what he'd prefer her to say.

Boyfriend? Nah.

Partner? Maybe.

Soul mate? That's what it felt like to him.

For the first time, he understood guys who introduced a woman as their wife and the pride that accompanied their declaration—equal parts possession, ego boost since they'd chosen you in return, and honor.

Maybe someday…

"Am I doing it wrong or something?" She tipped her head.

"Huh?"

"My attempt at seduction. I thought you'd be sprinting for the chopper at the promise of a BJ. I mean, I did say the *best* BJ ever, didn't I? Not one of those sloppy, half-assed, get it wet so you can put it in faster kind. I mean like the unreciprocated, lay back and enjoy—"

If she didn't stop talking, he was going to yank down his shorts right there.

So he lunged to his feet, snagged the backpack, then grabbed Sabine, too.

She laughed as he ran, carrying her, the entire length of the trail.

After he boosted her into their waiting ride, Miguel spoke quietly to Waverly, who had already loaded their bikes and moved on to her pre-flight checks. "When you radio in to Captain Alex with our flight details, can you please ask him to check out Brad Post, grad student at UoH. He's probably just some socially awkward bookworm, but he was poking around, asking Sabine a lot of questions about her work this morning. It's been bugging me ever since. Maybe we should add some security to her lab, too. Cameras, extra locks, stuff like that."

Of all people, Waverly would understand. Shit could turn ugly in an instant.

"Sure, Miguel." She put her hand on his forearm and squeezed. "Things are going to turn out okay."

"I know." He really did believe that.

After all, he didn't plan to let anything happen to Sabine. He'd waited a lifetime for the perfect woman to spend the rest of his life with. Now that he'd found her, he didn't intend to lose her.

THIRTEEN

Sabine couldn't wait for Waverly to whisk them back to the *Divemaster*. Maybe Miguel would take her to the clubroom and help her work off some of this naughty energy he'd had her stockpiling all damn day in his sexy, generous, romantic presence. If he didn't, she'd probably tackle him the moment they got back to their cabin.

Their cabin.

When had she started thinking of his space as her home?

She wasn't sure, but somewhere along the line she had. There was nowhere else she felt more comfortable, and not only because of the lavish amenities. Truthfully, as long as Miguel's arms were around her, holding her close to the steady thump of his heart, she'd make do.

Sabine glanced at Miguel and found him staring back at her with the same red-hot lust burning in his gaze. That would never get old.

"Hey, Waverly!" he called up to their badass lady pilot.

"Yeah?"

"Remember that time I helped you make Archie's underwater sex fantasy come true?"

He did what? Sabine wondered exactly how that worked and if they could try it sometime. She forgot to ask him, though, when he kept talking.

"How about you pay me back now?" He winked at Waverly while his hand wandered up Sabine's thigh, beneath the hem of her skirt.

"What'd you have in mind?" Waverly joked, "Kind of hard to have a threesome when I'm doing the flying. Besides, Archer would kill you."

"Very funny." Miguel chuckled. "I want you to roll up that partition and take a few laps around the island. I'll knock when we're ready to go home."

"We have an intercom, you know?" She grinned. "Pretend to be the worldly multi-millionaire you are, Miguel. Or at least act as if you're civilized."

"What fun would that be? Besides, we all know I'm asking for privacy because I'm going to fuck my date until she can hardly walk. Nothing refined about that, is there?" He poked around on the control panel by his seat, finding the button for the partition himself. "Toodles, Waverly."

The dainty finger wave he gave his best friend's girlfriend was so utterly ridiculous that both women burst out laughing.

Sabine's humor faded fast when he turned on her with his blue laser stare. "Strip."

"Like burlesque strip or like set-the-world-record-for-getting-naked strip? I'm not very coordinated, but

I could give the sexy variety a whirl if you've got some music…" It wasn't nervousness, exactly, that had her rambling. More like anticipation and the desire to be perfect for him. As wonderful as he was for her without trying.

"Ditch your clothes. Now." Though brusque, his gravelly command didn't alarm her. She'd been teasing him for hours. A man—or a woman for that matter—could only stand so much sweet torture in a single day.

"Oh. Right." Sabine toed off her sneakers and socks, wriggled out of her shorts and panties, then whipped her shirt and bra over her head. The necklace he'd given her stayed, as always. Without it she would feel naked in ways she'd never anticipated before. It comforted her, reminding her of his presence in her life. She understood the importance of talismans to some cultures much more after wearing his.

It carried an enchantment for her that she didn't ever want to go without again.

He seemed to wholly approve of her obsession with his gift.

"That's better." He admired her, bared completely to him. And she didn't mean only her nudity.

Miguel saw her clearly. He understood her moods, boosted her up when she was low, took charge when she longed to be free of responsibility for a little while, and never left her unsatisfied when she craved him. Like she did now.

"On your knees at my feet." He took her hand and tugged, helping her sink to the plush carpeting as he spread his thighs wide.

Sabine looked up at him, waiting for his direction.

"Undress me," he ordered.

She started with his sneakers, untying them and slipping them from his feet. It was unusual to see him wearing shoes of any kind since they weren't allowed on the precious decks of the *Divemaster*. When she peeled off his socks, revealing his tanned toes, she felt like she was uncovering the man she'd gotten to know so well.

Her hands trailed up his legs, the thick dark hair on them tickling her palms.

When she reached his shorts, skimming her fingers over the front of them, she intentionally goaded him before undoing the fly so that his already hard cock could spring free. His massive erection was framed by the canvas as it rested on his abdomen.

The resolve she'd had to go slow and steady flew out the window then.

Hell, she could climb into his lap and sink over his shaft in a matter of seconds if she hadn't promised him a world-class sucking.

Sabine rushed, shoving his shirt up before tugging it over his head and flinging it somewhere behind her. Then she yanked on his shorts.

He laughed as he lifted his fine ass from the seat so she could slip the last of his clothes from his body. "In a hurry?"

"Uh huh." She nodded, licking her lips.

"Tell me again about how you're going to give me the best blowjob of my life." He speared his fingers into her hair and brought her face close to his groin. Not close enough for her to taste him yet, though.

"Why don't you let me show you instead?" She peered up at him through the veil of her lashes as she asked for permission to suck his dick.

When he didn't respond right away, she begged, "Please. I want to taste you. Feel your heat and hardness on my tongue. And when you come, I want to know it's for me, because I've made you feel even a tiny bit as good as you've made me feel. Today especially. But since the moment I met you, really."

"Every day I spend with you is a happy one, *lindeza*." He brushed his thumb over her parted lips, dipping it inside for a split second, long enough for her to flick her tongue over the tip. "But go ahead. Suck my cock. Make today one for the record books."

She rocked forward, swallowing his length in a single long glide, not stopping until she had all of him wrapped in the heat and softness of her mouth. He prodded into her throat. Good thing she didn't have much of a gag reflex, because he had enough length and girth to be a serious choking hazard.

Either would have made his cock impressive.

Together, they made him God's gift to her pussy.

Sabine shivered as she began to suck on him, hoping later he might show her again how well they fit despite his decidedly above average endowment. She bobbed over him, paying special attention to the sensitive spot beneath his crown before sinking lower once more.

His fingers clenched in her hair and on her shoulder. Soon, he began to pump upward as she sank over him. The veins along his shaft grew more defined as his sac tightened in her palm.

"Sabine!" he called out for her as he reached the limits of his restraint. She didn't bother to slack off. Instead, she fluttered her tongue across the underside of his shaft and sucked harder on his tip at the apex of each stroke.

It was then that she felt the first gush of liquid coat her tongue, a precursor to his actual orgasm.

With one final plunge, she took him deep and swallowed around him.

Miguel roared as he came. His body arched, coiled as tightly as a loaded spear gun, before bursting into motion. His abs flexed as he emptied his balls down her throat, making her gulp to keep up with the pulses of his come.

Part of her pouted, just a little. He wouldn't leave her hanging. But even his spectacular pussy-eating or the dexterity of his fingers—or both of those things together, for that matter—couldn't get her off as well as the pounding of his cock within her.

"Don't stop sucking." He tapped her cheek when she slowed, preparing to let him slide from between her lips.

Her gaze snapped to his.

"Keep going and you'll have me hard again in a few minutes." He grinned wickedly then. "You didn't think I was going to pass up the opportunity to fuck you in a helicopter, did you?"

She shook her head, doing something that apparently felt great to his dick in the process. Whatever hint of firmness he'd lost after his orgasm began to return. The fat tip of his cock bumped against her palate. Damn, how did he do that? And how many times in a row could she make him come?

Sabine planned a naughty test for another day. Right now, she had to have him buried within her as quickly as possible. She hollowed her cheeks and increased the pressure on his shaft.

He groaned and thrust upward, nearly making her choke.

Redoubling her efforts, Sabine cupped his balls in her palm and rolled them lightly. A soft touch there never failed to arouse him. Today was no exception.

"Yes," he hissed. "Suck."

She did, bringing him back to full erection before long.

When her jaw had begun to ache, he lifted her to the seat and pushed her to her back. He crushed his mouth over hers, making her forget about any mild discomfort with swipes of his tongue and the brush of his lips.

While she ate at him, he fed her pussy his cock.

He pressed against her opening, working to penetrate as he always had to at first. But when he poked through the rings of muscle and spread them around his shaft, her body accommodated him. He hunched his back so that he could suck on her nipples as he began to turn the tables, raining rapture on her.

Because he'd already come, taken the edge off, he was able to pump into her relentlessly. Sabine couldn't resist that much direct stimulation. She felt her orgasm coalescing, barely out of reach.

Miguel clenched his ass tighter with every stroke, rubbing her clit with the root of his cock. It didn't take long before she was clawing at his back, whether to slow him down or egg him on, she couldn't say.

It didn't matter. He worked her as he pleased, which turned out to be exactly how she needed it. Hard and steady, with evenly spaced thrusts that her body began to anticipate.

One or two more strokes and she'd be past the point of no return.

Of course he knew that, too.

"Come, *lindeza.*" He kissed her then, swallowing her cries of completion. And only when she'd finally quit spasming around him did she realize he hadn't stopped fucking. "Do it again."

"I can't—"

"You will." He wouldn't accept any other outcome.

So she settled in and focused on the muted friction of his cock, which glided through the evidence of her arousal more easily now that he'd inspired her body to unleash one of the strongest waves of ecstasy she'd ever experienced. He never once paused as he kissed her, bringing her back to full arousal much more quickly than she would have thought possible.

When she was with him, moving against him to steal more pleasure from his body, he smiled.

Then he pulled out, though only long enough to roll her over.

He lifted her hips and helped her get into position so that one knee was on the seat while her other foot planted itself on the floor. Ass up, face pressed to the supple leather, she gasped when he reentered her from behind, then sank even deeper than before.

She was certain no one had ever been so far inside her. The thought alone spurred another orgasm. A violent one that only left her hungry for more right away. "Miguel!"

"Damn, Sabine," he panted as he blanketed her back and bit her shoulder. "That was amazing. I wanted better access to your clit, but I guess I didn't need it that time."

Still he fucked her, slow and steady as she caught her breath.

"Not when you hit right...there." She moaned when he tapped the spot inside her again. "Oh God. That's so good. So *deep.*"

"Going deep is my specialty," he growled.

"Miguel," she gasped. "Seriously, I think you're so far in me you might poke out my mouth soon."

He laughed at that, but didn't stop fucking. To have a man who could appreciate humor in bed without losing his hard-on or feeling threatened was a bonus. Sabine grinned against the seat. At least until he got serious real quick, adding the stroke of his thumb across her clit to the rock of his pelvis.

She didn't stand a chance at resisting when he played her like that.

He knew all her secrets by now.

Somehow, that didn't scare her as much as it should. In fact, it amplified the pleasure he bestowed with his fluid movements and the unrelenting drive of his cock within her.

"When you go over this time, I'm coming with you," he promised. "Almost there?"

The thought of him painting her with his release, marking her—even if it was inside, where no one else could see—was almost enough on its own to trigger her climax. "Yes."

"Good girl." He lifted his chest upright far enough to expose her ass a bit. She knew what he was about to do, but it didn't make it any less enjoyable when his palm connected with her cheek.

It only took three solid swats before she shattered.

Sabine muffled her scream against the seat as she unraveled.

The pulses of Miguel's hot come splattering against her over-sensitized tissue triggered wave after wave of spasms. Only when she was sure he'd flooded her pussy did he release his grip around her waist and withdraw his softening cock.

He held her in place with one palm at the base of her spine while he reached for his shirt and did his best to clean the trickles of semen that escaped to ice her thighs.

Sabine sighed, feeling like she might deflate or melt into a puddle on the spot.

"I didn't hurt you, did I?" he asked, serious for a moment.

"No, I like it when you go deep." Too bad he didn't realize just how far within her he'd tunneled. He'd wormed his way straight into her heart. Denying it any longer would be foolish.

In silence, they got dressed as best they could. Miguel stuffed his messy shirt in his backpack and finger-combed her hair into some semblance of order. The entire time, he kept staring into her eyes, as if he could see her soul. As deep as it was possible to get inside a human, she supposed.

"*Lindeza*, I lo—"

She sure wished the bolt of inspiration that had struck her then had waited a measly half-second longer. Because her imagination was trying to convince her that he had been about to drop the L-bomb when she interrupted with a shriek.

"Might want to take it easy, Miguel." Waverly's snark came over the intercom before she said, "Seriously, though. Everything all right back there? I thought you were finished. We don't have enough gas left for too many more rounds like that."

Miguel dropped the partition even as he stared at Sabine as though she might have lost her mind.

"Sorry!" She slapped her hand over her mouth. "It's just that you inspired a thought…"

"If it has to do with his cock or some freaky sex shit he was pulling on you, I don't want to hear about it." Waverly kept her eyes on the horizon as she aimed them toward the *Divemaster* and the rest of their friends.

"Maybe I had it wrong again." Sabine gestured with her hands, wishing they could read her mind. "What if the darkness Heinrich referred to wasn't caused by night at all."

"Depth?" Miguel's stare snapped to hers.

"His letter said something about digging deeper." She squinted as she pictured the email in her mind. "'Until you change the way you look at things—blind yourself to what you think you know and dig a little deeper—you might never see it.'"

"Hmm." Miguel tapped his chin. "There aren't that many parts of the crater interior that are very deep.

Certainly none enough to cause perpetual darkness. But…"

"What is it?" Sabine turned in her seat to face him, clasping his hands in hers. "Nothing is too out there—he was telling me to think outside the box."

"What if we think outside the crater instead?" Miguel peered at the sea. He pointed to Molokini. "See how the water changes color on the backside, shifting from turquoise to navy?"

"Yes," she and Waverly said in unison.

"It's deep over there. The far side of the islet drops straight down to at least three hundred and fifty feet. With strong currents. Advanced divers drop in there. Their boats take off to the opposite end of the island and pick them up after they drift along the entire length." He looked at her then, his pupils dilating.

"What?"

"The other reason people avoid it—or seek it out—is because it's in constant shadow."

Sabine felt the familiar rush of hope. This time she was too afraid to embrace it fully.

"And if you go a bit farther out, off the shelf, the bottom falls away rapidly in the Alalakeiki Channel to twice that easily," he explained.

"That's deep enough to be around the bottom of the disphotic zone or maybe even to the top of the aphotic zone." She tapped her chin as she considered the possibilities.

"What does that mean?" Waverly asked as she began their descent to the *Divemaster*.

"It's very close to the limit light from the surface can reach. Worth a try to investigate, but way too deep for us to dive and collect samples from if there are even any deep sea corals down there," Miguel answered for her.

Sabine nodded. "I know this is kind of crazy…but you don't happen to have a submarine lying around in your stash of billionaire toys, do you?"

Waverly jumped in to help. "With Archer's money and my connections in the Navy, I bet we can scrounge up a DSV to borrow. That's a Deep Submergence Vehicle for you non-military acronym types. And you know, by *we*…I mean *Banks*. He can sweet-talk anyone. Besides, he's becoming a pro at writing donation checks."

Miguel laughed. "He's going to love this."

⤳ FOURTEEN ⤳

Sabine stood on the launch deck of the *Divemaster* less than a week later, blown away by what true wealth could do. What if everyone who'd somehow amassed a personal fortune used theirs for the benefit of others, like Archer did?

To secure use of a DSV from Woods Hole Oceanographic Institution on her own would have taken her years of grant writing, which would have required support from top quality research papers with far more promising results as initial proof than she currently had. Even if by some miracle she could have made it that far, it might have taken another couple of years to assemble a qualified team and book their field time, which would have been extremely limited.

Probably less than the length of time she'd already spent on the *Divemaster*.

Which meant they might have failed, walked away from whatever was waiting for them below the surface. And after so much time had passed—five years minimum—maybe whatever it was Heinrich had found would have moved on or disappeared forever.

This had to work. She would never have a better opportunity than this.

Miguel stood shoulder to shoulder with her as someone from the DSV's permanent crew trained them on how to pilot the personal submarine. "Honestly, it's unbelievably simple. You just use the joystick. If you've ever played videogames, you're probably set."

"Dibs on driving," Miguel said to her.

"Fine with me." She figured she'd be too busy gawking at their surroundings to be of much use in that department.

"I'll also have redundant controls," the sub crewman told them. "I can handle things from the surface if you aren't comfortable once you're down there. I'll also be backup in case something breaks on your dashboard. This is a shallow mission for this kind of vehicle. A walk in the park compared to some of the places we've visited, like the Mariana Trench. I'll essentially be able to see everything you see and can even operate the collection arms and the slurp gun, which will suck up specimens without harming them. So if you prefer, I can take over and you can just sit back and enjoy the ride."

They both nodded at that, glad for the support.

"I can't believe we're really going to do this," Sabine murmured to Miguel.

"I know. It's going to be one of the top ten most amazing things I've ever done in my life." Leaning in closer he whispered, "Right up there with fucking you."

Sabine rolled her eyes.

"Do that again and I'll have you over my knee in the clubroom later. I'm not joking." He kissed her temple, then returned his attention to the researcher. "So when can we be ready to go?"

"Frankly, anytime." He shrugged. "We've checked the launch area and conditions are ideal today. Calm and clear. You don't have to worry about racing the daylight since you're going deep anyway."

"I don't want to wait." Sabine had a nagging sense that they were running out of time.

"Let's give the rest of the crew a one-hour warning." Miguel asked, "Will that work?"

Sabine and the DSV handler both nodded.

Fifty-nine minutes later, Captain Alex had brought the ship into position. Banks, Tosin, Waverly, and Archer were on the sidelines of the launch deck lending moral support. Sabine had come to think of them not only as Miguel's friends, but as her own also.

Their guests lined the rails on the decks above, curious about the unusual addition to today's agenda. With so many eyes on her, Sabine felt the pressure building.

Rather than stand there and let it ramp up her apprehension, she wandered over toward Tosin and patted his back. "It's killing you not to get to play with it, isn't it?"

"I think if you need to make another trip under, you should rotate your assistants for fresh eyes." He'd been trying for days to weasel into a mission.

"Fair enough." She smiled up at him. "But you have to tell Miguel."

"Tell me what?" He joined them, having finished the last of his briefings with the ship's staff.

"I'm getting a turn in that thing one way or another." Tosin grinned. "Don't make me resort to joyriding in the middle of the night. You know I will."

Banks closed his eyes and shook his head. "I have no desire to deal with that much paperwork."

Sabine found herself laughing, completely at ease within seconds. More each day, she felt she belonged here. With them. What happened in the next couple of hours would likely change her life forever, one way or another.

She hoped it ended up for the better.

"Dr. Reynolds, we're set!" the DSV crew lead called to her.

Banks stepped forward first, hugging each of them. Waverly, Archer, and even Tosin followed suit. He crushed her in his embrace. "Have a safe trip."

"Thank you." Her throat tightened, making anything else she might have said impossible to get out.

Hand in hand, she and Miguel approached the DSV, which looked like a giant glass bubble with canary-yellow legs, almost cartoony in its odd proportions. They climbed in, Miguel first to give him more room, then her. When the hatch was closed and locked behind them, she jumped.

"Things are starting to feel pretty damn real, huh?" Miguel looked at her, reading her reaction.

"Yeah." She hoped he knew she counted their growing connection in that agreement.

They strapped in to the bucket seats and waited for the crane to lift them over the edge. Miguel held her hand as the countdown commenced over the radio.

"Three...two..."

And then they were freefalling a dozen or so feet into the ocean, where they landed with a sploosh worthy of a blue whale doing a belly flop.

Sabine cheered even though her stomach had executed some Olympic-level flips in the process. Miguel hooted right along with her as bubbles skated in front of the submarine's viewing window.

She had come to accept that it would be like this for them. Even in the midst of one of the most important expeditions of her career, he was there with her. A part of it, fully engaged. And if he was there, that meant they were going to enjoy each other and the time they spent together while they could.

It didn't mean she cared less about her work.

It meant she cared more about him.

"I take it from that reaction that you're both fine after entry?" the DSV's crewleader asked.

"Yes!" Sabine shouted, somewhat breathless from the rush.

"Beginning descent," he droned, taking things much more seriously than they were. She was glad someone responsible was watching their backs. In truth, there wasn't much for them to do except hang on and peer out the window, looking for who-knew-what.

They'd agreed to start their quest at the site called Edge of the World since the notch in the back wall of Molokini was well known for casting shadows on itself; that meant it existed in perpetual darkness. From there they would comb the wall. If they still hadn't found anything, they'd zigzag out to the trench.

With a maximum bottom time of ten hours, they started checking off squares on the search grid. For the most part, there was a lot of not much to be seen.

Humpback whales were common in this part of the ocean, though not typical at this time of year. Sabine couldn't imagine staring through their bubble into the giant eye of a creature that size. Especially not one as intelligent as a whale. That would be a treat in itself.

A few bluefin trevallys buzzed past on the hunt for smaller, unsuspecting fish. They also spotted a giant barracuda and a couple of white-tipped reef sharks in the distance. But none of the corals here were different than the ones they'd already studied.

They took their time, collecting a half-dozen samples just to be sure before moving deeper.

As the light continued to fade, Sabine started to lose faith.

There weren't any deep-sea corals known to live in this area. They were going to look anyway.

The DSV followed the crack in the cliff deeper, deeper, deeper.

Back on the *Divemaster*, Tosin barked out their depth in hundreds of feet. They kept ticking away. Thinking of the weight of the entire ocean pressing in around them caused her breath to come in short blasts.

"It's okay." Miguel squeezed her hand. "You heard the expert. This thing is designed to go way deeper than this."

She nodded. "It just seems so...desolate down here. I know it's not. There are squid and microorganisms, and who knows what else. Compared to where we've been diving for the past month, though, it's like night and day."

"And even this is probably teeming with life compared to some of the vast expanses of uncharted territory in some places of the world. Sometimes I get the feeling people think the entire ocean is like the parts they see right offshore. Maybe if more of them realized the density of wildlife is actually disproportionally dispersed, they would think twice about taking so much from the sea unsustainably."

Sabine completely agreed.

"We're nearing the bottom," Miguel said, partially for their friends back on the *Divemaster*, as he read the radar screen. It had taken them more than four hours to get there. Not because they couldn't have gone faster if they'd taken a direct route, but because they'd been working along the whole cliff face, determined not to miss a thing.

"Are my eyes catching reflections from the instruments on the viewing window again or do you see..." She squinted, trying to make sense of the faint bluish glow coming from below them.

It got more intense by the second.

"It's not you." Miguel sat forward, peering beneath the DSV as best he could.

She flipped through the various camera feeds on the display embedded in the dashboard until she found the one she was looking for. And when she did, Sabine could only stare in shock.

"What *is* that?" she whispered.

Miguel replied, "My best guess would be some sort of bioluminescent algae that uses an internal chemical reaction to create light. It seems to be concentrated on those rocks over there."

He guided the research vessel closer to the phenomenon. Over the radio, people back on the *Divemaster*—researchers and boat staff alike—were losing their minds. Gasps and shouts, even some clapping, were clearly audible over the speakers.

As they approached, Sabine detected a shimmer in the water and the DSV's sensors noted an increase in temperature.

"There's a good-sized hydrothermal vent down here." Miguel came to the same conclusion she did at precisely the same time.

And still Sabine sat there, unblinking, unmoving. She didn't make a peep.

"Why aren't you freaking out right now? Jumping up and down or screaming?" he asked. "Something."

"Because I'm scared." She tried not to let him see the tears that began to stream down her cheeks. Of course he noticed, and wiped them away. He focused on her while she kept looking at the flickering lights that danced before them.

"Of what?" He rested his non-driving hand on her thigh.

"If this isn't what Heinrich was working on, I can't imagine what the hell it might have been." After a month of false hope and disappointment, she wasn't sure she could believe again or survive another disappointment.

Miguel was silent for a moment as they both stared, in awe of the bizarre environment almost no one else had ever witnessed. Except maybe Heinrich. Fairly certain he'd somehow been in precisely this spot, she felt closer to his memory. At times like these she was reminded how little humanity understood about the place they called home. She hoped they could figure out the critical stuff before they ruined it.

Gears whirred and the teams above began using remote operations to gently collect their samples. While they worked, she started scribbling observations in her journal.

She noted that the edges of the glowing algae bed didn't seem quite as vibrant as the rest. Die off seemed to have shrunk the mass of algae by as much as a third recently enough that she could tell where it had once reached. With rising ocean temperatures, increasing pollution, and the introduction of radioactivity from the Fukushima nuclear disaster not *too* far from here on an oceanic scale, who knew what kind of undiscovered organisms were on the verge of extinction?

If this one turned out to be some miracle cure for one of the most prevalent diseases on their planet, could they harvest enough to start growing it in a lab? What if the rest of this colony disappeared before they could figure how to maintain the conditions it needed to thrive?

To have discovered a solution to the cancer crisis only to have it slip away...that would be a catastrophe.

Sort of like if you'd fallen completely in love with a man then had to give him up.

Miguel sat still, letting her process her thoughts as if he felt as reverent as she did in this moment. After a few minutes, the machines beneath them fell quiet.

They had what they'd come for.

Finally, she turned toward Miguel. He deserved her honesty. "I'm also terrified that this might be the thing we've been searching for. If it is...then what? Where does that leave us?"

He shushed her. "We'll figure it out."

What did that even mean?

How could she be involved in the years of research and development it would take to turn a raw material into a viable drug without either leaving Miguel or forcing him to abandon his own fulfilling life's work?

Neither of them would be happy if they sacrificed their careers for the other.

"Come here." He released her harness and tugged until she'd landed in his lap. It was a tight squeeze, but manageable.

Miguel put his arms around her then kissed her. "For now, let's celebrate the incredible things we've seen together already. Who gets a chance like this?"

"To discover something groundbreaking?" she clarified.

Is this what Jonas Salk had felt like when he cured polio? Or Louis Pasteur when he'd developed a vaccine for rabies? To think that someday people might remember Heinrich—or maybe even her and Miguel—like one of those pioneers blew her mind.

"No, *lindeza*. The chance to have sex in a sub." He grinned. "If Tosin thought he was jealous before, wait until that sucker finds out we joined the mile deep club."

✧ FIFTEEN ✧

Sabine filled their tiny space with peals of her laughter. While Miguel loved the sound of it, he hadn't been kidding in the slightest. From the pad in front of him, he peeled off a sticky note and put it over the lens of the interior cabin camera.

"What are you doing?" Sabine asked, her eyes growing even wider than they'd been when she'd spotted the glow of the blue algae.

"I told you. I'm about to fuck you in a sub. Going deep has never sounded so good." He winked. "So hike up that skirt and let's see just how flexible you are. There's not a lot of room to spare here but I think we can get the job done."

Before she could protest, Miguel tapped the transmit button on the radio and said, "Surface control, we're having a minor glitch. Could you take the wheel for a minute?"

"Yeah, I see we just lost a camera, too. All other systems are green light, though. I've got you covered. Don't panic." The operator's cool, professional tone only made what they were about to do more illicit and a little risky.

If his cock hadn't already been hard, it would have pumped up in a hurry with that added edge of rebelliousness.

He thought he might have to persuade Sabine, but he should have known better. She'd already started squeezing around instruments to orient herself properly in his lap, willing and eager to join him on yet another adventure. Hopefully, he could make it good for her.

"Sorry, we don't have more than a couple minutes at most." He unzipped his shorts and took out his cock.

Sabine kissed him as she put one knee on either side of his thighs, careful not to squash his balls in the process of contorting herself into a position that would allow her to ride him. Miguel put two fingers up, letting her suck on them to get them nice and wet.

When he shoved the crotch of her panties aside and rubbed them against her pussy, he found he hadn't needed to. She was already slick.

"Damn, *lindeza.*" He kissed her neck alongside his necklace, which was conveniently at mouth level.

"Yeah. I guess playing explorer turns me on. Who knew?" She let her head fall back so that he could lick and nip the sensitive spot below her ear. The motion turned her hair into golden streamers, making his hands itch to twist it up and use it to tug her onto his waiting shaft.

So he did.

Unlike the long, drawn-out lovemaking they'd indulged in most nights, this was something different. Fast and hard. Kind of desperate. It was everything he felt at the moment, knowing her time with him might be drawing quickly to a close.

Sabine guided his cock, angling it so that she could take as much as possible given their cramped quarters. She fit him to her opening then dropped, burying him several inches deep in a single thrust. She cried out, and not entirely in pleasure.

"Slow down." He held onto her waist, keeping her from impaling herself farther.

She shoved at him, bearing down and taking him bit by bit. "No. It's fine. Kind of hurts, but I like it."

He rewarded her honesty with a flex of his ass and abs, driving upward even as she sank some more. Sabine gasped. Her hands landed on his shoulders, clinging to him as she began to raise and lower herself, screwing him deeper within her pussy with every swing of her hips.

Having her on top, setting her free to use him to bring herself pleasure, had its perks. He settled back and enjoyed the view: Sabine, the rarely seen landscape, and the glimmering illumination provided by the algae decorating the rocks along the seabed.

It was almost otherworldly, this experience.

Miguel let his head rest against the seat and Sabine took advantage, leaning forward to kiss him. He let her have anything she wanted from him. Everything she could take.

She rode him hard enough that the sub rocked slightly. He found the motion comforting, arousing even. On the open seas or under them, with her was where he'd always like to be.

When her pussy began to tighten around him, he knew this moment couldn't last forever.

"Rub your clit," he rasped. "I'm not coming without you."

Watching her manipulate herself while using his cock to get off was one of the hottest things he'd ever seen. He clenched his jaw and waited for the telltale clamp of her muscles and the soft mewling sounds she made as she got close to orgasm.

He could listen to that on constant repeat.

"That's right, *lindeza*," Miguel urged her, thrusting upward with short jabs as her own motions became jerky and erratic. "Concentrate on the pleasure. Feel me inside you."

Sabine's eyes flew open then. She stared right into his as she surrendered to the passion they generated together. He crushed his lips over hers as she moaned and came, slathering his cock with her release.

His body reacted in turn, feeding off of her ecstasy.

Come launched from his balls in several long, violent blasts that relieved the ache in his groin, but made him more aware of the one in his heart.

It wouldn't matter what end of the earth he searched—how high the mountains he climbed or how deep the oceans he scanned—he'd never find another woman like Sabine.

No one else could do this to him.

Miguel kissed her softly, smiling as she recovered enough to lift off of him and resituate herself on her side of the DSV. He checked his watch. It wasn't often he was proud of getting the job done in less than two minutes.

This was one of them.

Hey, a great fuck was a great fuck, no matter how long it took. He held his hand up to Sabine and she returned his high five. After zipping up, he leaned forward and pressed the radio transmit button. "Hello? Can you hear us?"

"Loud and clear," Captain Alex answered.

"Sorry, must have had some technical difficulties there for a few minutes. We've got what we need and are beginning our ascent now."

The captain coughed to cover what sounded like a chuckle. "That might be easier to believe if Sabine's ass hadn't been planted on the transmitter while you were nailing her, kid. Sounded like a helluva lot of fun, though. Now get back here before something really does break and we have to haul you out."

Miguel burst out laughing. He wasn't about to apologize. Anyone else would have done the same thing in his place. Sabine, even with her cheeks now flaming, was gorgeous and supremely fuckable.

"Thanks for the Sub Fucking 101 advice. See you on the surface." This time Miguel was careful to take his hand completely away from the radio when he spoke privately to Sabine. "Sorry about that."

She shrugged, surprisingly okay with being busted. "I guess the past month has made me realize that doing your job well and having fun are in no way mutually exclusive."

"Very true. I've always loved being a divemaster. I'd do it for free if I had to." Miguel practically *had* done it for free for years. Living simply hadn't bothered him in the least.

"You were meant for this. You belong here." She smiled sadly then looked out their giant bubble window.

He didn't like the sound of that. "I'm starting to think that I belong wherever you are."

"Don't, Miguel." She shook her head. "We haven't made any promises to each other for a reason."

"I guess." He hated it, but she was right about that.

That didn't mean he didn't wish they could. Or wish that they were in a position where things would work out if they did.

"This would be a pretty baller way to propose to someone, though." He tossed it out there casually, as if he wasn't pissed that he didn't have a ring in his pocket to give Sabine right then. Maybe if he had, he would've been able to talk her into staying before the realities waiting for them back on the surface crashed over them with the destructive force of a tsunami.

Hopefully it wouldn't wipe out the progress they'd made or the bond they'd formed so far.

He didn't place very good odds on that when she didn't respond at all.

They spent the rest of the return journey holding hands, but in silence.

∾ SIXTEEN ∾

Sabine stood in her makeshift laboratory, which had never been this crowded before. Besides herself, Miguel, Tosin, Archer, Waverly, Banks, and Captain Alex, a couple people from WHOI packed like sardines into the space. Plus, her laptop was open. Marta's head floated on the screen as she joined them remotely.

No pressure.

She'd worked in a few of the top facilities in the world, but nothing would ever replace this nook of the *Divemaster* as her favorite place to work. So she had mixed emotions about what she was hoping for as she watched seconds ticking by on her stopwatch.

"This is as bad as waiting on a damn pregnancy test," Waverly muttered from beside her. "Staring at that indicator trying to convince yourself you see lines, or don't see lines, depending. I'll stick to flying, thanks."

Sabine laughed and turned to her friend. "At least I didn't pee on myself. Well, I haven't yet anyway. We'll see when these results—"

DING!

That simple sound nearly stopped Sabine's heart. She froze. Everyone stared at her.

"Go ahead, *lindeza*." Miguel nudged her toward the sample.

She prepped the slide and took it to the microscope. Before she looked through it, she scanned the room. Banks flashed her a thumbs-up. Optimism. Hope. Unwavering support. They radiated positivity and encouragement.

Marta especially. If she could be strong enough to do this, Sabine had to live up to that standard. She drew a deep breath then put her face against the eyepiece. It took a second to bring the specimen into focus.

When she did...

Sabine thought she might pass out. She gripped the countertop as if it were the only thing holding her upright then looked again. And a third time, just to be sure.

If she hadn't prepared the sample herself, she wouldn't have believed what she saw.

Not only had the cancerous cells been destroyed, but the healthy tissue appeared completely intact, something modern medicine hadn't been able to master after decades of research. Until now.

No. Until a few months ago, when Heinrich had seen this very same thing. She was sure of it.

Sabine couldn't hold her emotions in check another moment. She lost it. Completely. Though she wasn't normally the kind of person to burst into tears, she did it for the second time that day.

She cried so hard she couldn't breathe.

Miguel raced to her side and held her tight. "It's okay, Sabine. We'll try again. There are more samples to test."

"No—" She couldn't get more out than that.

"I'll search every ocean on Earth with you if that's what it takes. We'll do this. Together." He held her tighter, breaking her heart more with every amazingly kind word he spoke. Because she knew she wouldn't be able to commit to him in the face of what she'd just seen.

"Miguel, stop," she begged.

As if he was thinking of their time in the clubroom like she was, he didn't say another word. Instead, he peered down at her, waiting.

"It worked."

"What's happening?" Marta asked from the laptop. "Is Sabine okay?"

"Are you serious?" Either Sabine was shaking hard enough to move them both or Miguel was trembling along with her.

She nodded. "It's...incredible."

Miguel put his hands around her ribs, his thumbs below her breasts, and lifted her high above his head. He spun her around and around, then shouted, "You did it!"

When he put her down, everyone surged forward, encapsulating them both in one giant group hug. Through the ruckus, she heard Marta thanking some nameless entity in German.

"*I* didn't do it. Heinrich did." Sabine would be diligent about making sure any credit for the discovery was correctly attributed to him.

"Don't short yourself. You didn't have to pursue this. You could have quit after the string of failures. But you didn't." Miguel took her shoulders in his hands then and stared directly into her eyes so that she couldn't dismiss what he was saying. "I'm honored to be able to say that the woman I love did something so impressive. Something that will improve millions of lives. I'm proud of you, Sabine."

"Wait, what did you say?" She blinked up at him.

"That I'm in awe of your accomplishments? How could you possibly doubt that?" he wondered.

"I don't." Her eyes were filling with tears yet again. After this she'd get her shit together, she swore.

Tosin helped out. "She's talking about the part where you admitted that you love her. Although, it's not exactly a secret, is it? We figured that out a while ago."

Archer and Waverly were beaming at them and Banks nodded softly to himself, as if he wholly approved of Miguel's choice.

"Me too." Miguel kept dropping weights on Sabine—good and bad, good and bad—balancing the scales between elation and heartbreak. "From the moment I spotted her trudging through the airport, on her way to do what was right despite her broken heart, I knew on some level that I wanted a person like that in my life."

"I appreciate how much you've given me during this time. How you kept me going even on the toughest days." She hugged him tight.

"So what do we do now?" He asked the question she'd been dreading since they'd seen the blue shimmer in the deep. "It seems like we need to make some kind of announcement. Call CNN. Something like that. Right?"

"No!" Marta shouted at the same time Banks did, as if they were parents scolding a child playing too close to a busy road.

Sabine cringed. "I'm not sure that's wise. Heinrich kept this a secret—even mostly from me since he didn't trust communications to be secure—for a reason. He was the smartest person I've ever met. That explosion in his lab was no accident. I'm sure of it now. What we have here is practically priceless. I think we need to protect ourselves before making any public disclosures."

"I think that's best." Marta backed Sabine up, a hint of fear in her declaration.

"Then considering how late it already is here, and that it's the middle of the night in most of the rest of the country, maybe we should go celebrate then figure out our next steps in the morning." Archer stirred everyone up when he announced, "Champagne is on the way!"

A few hours later, after indulging in one glass more than it took to make her dizzy, Sabine craved the quiet, softly lit interior of the cabin she shared with Miguel.

"Ready to head to bed?" he asked.

"Mmm." She practically purred.

"Not like that." He laughed and kissed the tip of her nose. "I think you've had a little too much to drink."

Sabine pouted.

"Besides, I hope you don't mind but I kind of want to enjoy some quiet time with you."

Before you leave me.

He didn't say that last part. They both knew it was hanging there in the air between them anyway.

"Let's go." Sabine took his hand. She gladly accepted hugs, kisses, and cheers from each of the remaining people in her laboratory as the party dissolved along with the exit of the guest of honor. After she'd made her rounds, they strolled to their quarters, stripped at the door, and practically fell into bed.

After a slightly awkward silence, Miguel blurted, "What if I come with you?"

"Huh?" Sabine sat up, crossing her legs.

"You're going to need to file patents, do clinical trials, give lectures, and whatever other junk I don't even know about. You'll need a real lab and a home base that's not always moving or in some remote, unreachable place. But the only thing I need is you."

She tried to respond a few times and couldn't find the right way to say what she was thinking. "I'm not sure that you belong in my world, Miguel."

He jerked as if she'd slapped him. "The fuck I don't. I might not have ever made it to college, but I've learned all about you. Enough to know we fit together. In the morning, I'll show you just how well. I'll make it impossible for you to deny."

"It's not always about sex, Miguel." She tried to explain what she'd truly meant. "Of course, I don't disagree. That's the best I've ever had. Ever will have, I'm sure. And while I have no doubt you could fit in where I'm from, *this* is where you belong. With Archer and Tosin, diving all the time."

"I think I should get to decide that for myself," he insisted.

"Except that I've already thought about this a million different ways, Miguel." She tensed, her buzz rapidly disappearing. "I can't be your everything. I can't replace your beloved ocean. And when you're unhappy, locked with me in the glaring lights of a lab instead of the warm rays of the sun, you'll start to resent me from taking you away from your first love. I won't do that to you, Miguel."

"What you're doing by leaving me behind is worse," he snapped. Already proving her point. This wasn't how she wanted things between them to be. It was better to remember the perfect times they'd shared already than to ruin those memories with a bitter breakup.

Sabine hung her head, defeated.

"Hey, I'm sorry." Miguel put his hand on her shoulder and rubbed his thumb back and forth across the bare skin there. "I'm certain I don't want to spend whatever time we have together right now arguing."

She raised her hand across her body to her shoulder and squeezed his fingers. "Me either."

"So come here and let me hold you. We can worry about the rest tomorrow, after we've slept on things and have clear heads." He pulled her backward, so she didn't fight, tumbling to the bed they'd shared for a while now.

It was one of the very few times they didn't fool around before calling it a night. Cuddling with Miguel, listening to his breathing slow down and even out, relaxed her even if it filled her with profound grief. Because she could already clearly see her path, and it led far away from here, from him, and from the *Divemaster*.

From everything she'd come to love.

SEVENTEEN

Sabine tossed and turned. Despite Miguel's heat and hardness beside her, she couldn't quiet her mind long enough to drift off. She'd even found out that he snored, if lightly. Every other night she'd spent by his side she'd been well and truly unconscious—exhausted from the physical demands of diving and the mental burden of stress. Plus she'd been under the influence of a solid afterglow, which made a phenomenal biochemical sleep aid.

After what felt like an hour or two of torturing herself—the thing she wanted most within arm's reach and still totally unattainable—she swung her legs over the side of the mattress and sighed.

For a while longer, she watched Miguel sleep. Even unconscious he was one hell of a man—built, handsome, and surprisingly trusting given his upbringing. She thought of all the times he'd called her beautiful and figured he had that one wrong. *He* was the gorgeous one—inside and out—though he probably wouldn't appreciate her assessment if she shared it with him.

She kissed her fingers then pressed them lightly to his lips before rising.

His discarded *Got Air?* T-shirt draped over the desk chair. She lifted it to her nose and breathed in his scent, maybe crossing the line into creepy stalker territory, but she didn't give a shit. She might not have the chance to do weird stuff like that soon.

Sabine tugged his shirt on. It came nearly to her knees despite her being taller than average. She hugged herself, then slipped from the room with one final glance over her shoulder.

She murmured, "I love you, too, Miguel."

Then shut the door as quietly as possible.

Wandering along the hallway while most everyone else dreamed, Sabine trailed her fingertips over the shiny exotic woods and took time to really observe each of the art pieces in the crannies she'd strode past daily. Suddenly she had the desire to slow down and soak it all in.

Say goodbye.

Eventually, Sabine found herself reclining on one of the dive bay benches. She could see hints of Miguel everywhere. The neatly wrapped hoses he coiled just so. His wetsuit hanging up to dry outside his locker. The heart Tosin had drawn around her and Miguel's names on the whiteboard they used to record their dive plans for the day.

Would she be erased from the *Divemaster* as easily as her name could be wiped from that surface? Would Miguel start fresh with some new guest as soon as she had moved on?

Sabine slapped her hand on her thigh then continued her slow-motion tour, stepping into her laboratory. She flicked on the lights and came face to face with a man dressed entirely in black.

"Holy shit!" She recoiled, grasping her chest. By the time her synapses began firing enough to scream for her to make a run for it, it was too late.

The intruder wrapped one arm around her upper chest and put his hand over her mouth. "I thought you would never get up. Saved me a trip inside, though—thanks."

Sabine didn't have any formal training in self-defense. She had never been in the military like Waverly. But she had learned to fend for herself at an early age. More importantly, she had already been in the kind of mood that made her appreciate someone to punish.

Raw anger seeped from her every pore. She snarled and gnashed her teeth, biting the bastard's hand, hard. At the same time, she thrashed. Flailing elbows and knees and heels might not have been artfully aimed. They were, however, fueled by some of the most brutal emotions she'd ever experienced.

One of her wild stabs connected with something soft and hopefully really sensitive. Her attacker doubled over, letting her go. Sabine dashed through the door.

And was met with three more guys as sinister looking as the first.

Fuck.

She drew in a huge breath, ready to scream at the top of her lungs for help when one of the intruders stepped forward and jabbed a needle in her neck, directly into some major blood vessel. It was hard to say which because the world grew wobbly and unfocused almost immediately.

Sounds distorted, and she dropped to the deck boards.

The men were professional enough to get right to business, ignoring her for the most part. They began to trash the laboratory as she tried to orient herself and crawl to stop them from causing any irreparable damage to her equipment or her test result cultures.

Sabine wished she could do anything to delay them. From her spot on the ground she could see the security cameras Banks had installed overhead after they'd returned from their date day on Maui. Who was watching? Would someone be coming to save her even if it was too late for her samples?

She tried again to shout. Or stand. Or...do anything but slump uselessly on the floor.

It was pointless. Her arms and legs weren't cooperating with her brain's scrambled directives. And her disorientation only worsened by the second.

Glass shattered, computers were smashed, and when they'd done their worst, they lit the entire thing on fire. The initial whoosh of the flames singed her brows, filling her nose with the acrid smell of burning hair.

"Time to go," one of the men said as he hauled her up by her hair.

"What the fuck is going on here?" a familiar voice roared a moment before Tosin charged into view.

No! Sabine screamed, though only in her mind. Her mouth had stopped working.

Though he was a total badass, he couldn't possibly fend off the men now crawling over the dive bay like a pile of bristleworms. When he realized how serious these guys were, and that some shouting and bright lights weren't about to chase them off, he swung around to a supply cabinet. When he withdrew his hands he held an air horn in one and a multi-shot flare gun in the other.

He'd done a hell of a lot better than her in the thinking on his feet department.

Her vision blurred further. Still, she managed to get the gist of his attack when the air horn rent the night. Hopefully it would also draw more help. When the disposable can was empty, he threw it at one of the guys he was fighting off. The attacker stumbled, but kept coming.

Next, Tosin leveled the signal gun at one of the men charging him and fired. *BANG! BANGBANG!*

That took care of a few guys. More took their places.

Right about then the fire alarms began to wail. The suppression system that kicked in wouldn't do her laboratory any good. Everything was already ruined.

But things only got worse when Miguel charged into the fray.

If Tosin had thought on his feet, using the tools around him, Miguel operated on pure testosterone and fury. He pummeled his opponents with his fists in a sequence of altercations that had her head spinning even more.

Sabine got as far as her knees, trying to reach him, when someone kicked her in the ribs, putting her down and out once more. He got right in her face and screamed, "Tell us where the stuff is! We've looked all over this damn place for months. Where the fuck is it?"

She couldn't have answered if she wanted to. Her tongue was a brick in her mouth.

"I think you gave her too much of that shit," the man snarled, then picked her up. "We'll have to take her with us if we want answers."

Oh fuck no.

Blackness encroached on Sabine's vision. She fought, but nothing happened. Except that they toted her to the dive platform and tossed her onto a waiting speedboat below.

From her new position she couldn't see Miguel. She sure as shit heard him, though, as he fought his way to her. With one last effort, she managed to groan and lurch toward him.

"Knock his ass out and take him too," someone said. "That's her boyfriend. He'll be useful for making her talk."

It didn't take long before Miguel had been overpowered, completely outnumbered.

When he hit the bottom of the boat beside her, blood trickling down his face, his eyes open, she freaked the fuck out. Was he dead? Had they killed him because of her?

She could never forgive herself for that.

Sabine slumped slightly in his direction, ecstatic that her jarring motion roused him if only enough for him to groan and prove that he was alive.

Men leapt onto the boat, surrounding them.

From the *Divemaster*, Sabine thought she heard Captain Alex shouting orders. Soon it was impossible to tell over the noise the engine made when the bad guys opened up the throttle and drove them through the night to some unknown hellhole.

◦⊃ EIGHTEEN ⊂◦

Miguel paced the brig of whatever pirate ship he'd been stashed on. He only got in a couple steps before he had to turn around, but sitting there doing nothing had been driving him insane. Especially when he could see Sabine, crumpled on the floor of the cell across the hall, but couldn't reach her. She hadn't responded to any of his shouts either.

Please, let her be alive.

From the time he burst into the dive bay and was greeted by flames, things had been kind of a blur, but he thought he'd seen her watching him as he took out as many of the intruders on the *Divemaster* as he could. Unfortunately it hadn't been enough, and by the time he came to, in this damn prison cell, he had no idea what had happened past then, or what those bastards had done to Sabine.

The only thing giving him hope at the moment was that she was far more valuable alive, given her knowledge of Heinrich's operations and the methodology he used for his experiments. Then again...why had they burned her lab?

He didn't have to wait long to find out.

Some surprisingly normal-looking dude in a crisp shirt and well-tailored slacks approached their cells. He smiled at Miguel then barked orders to two of the hired muscles that followed a few steps behind. "Wake her up. We don't have much time. Those bastards on the megayacht are going to have the authorities here soon. It has to be done before they arrive."

Miguel could only imagine that their lives were about to go from bad to worse, but he still thanked every power in the universe that Sabine was still alive.

One of the goons opened her cell then reached inside. He kicked her.

Miguel roared and slammed his shoulder into the barred door of his cage. He knew it wouldn't do any good, but he couldn't overrule the primal part of his brain from insisting that he act on her behalf. They would pay for that.

When Sabine grunted and tried to fight back, though sleepily, a flare of pride rose in Miguel. Even under the influence of potent drugs, she was a fighter. They might still have a chance at escaping if they kept calm. A slim chance...

"This one could be some fun. Can we have her when you're done with her?" the guard taunted, staring at Miguel as he asked the boss.

"I may keep her for myself," he answered, also trying to read Miguel's expression.

He made it simple for them by flashing his middle fingers.

If they gave him a chance, he'd do a lot more than that.

Before things could deteriorate even further, Sabine came alert enough to cry out for him. "Miguel!"

"I'm here, *lindeza*. Stay calm."

She whipped her head toward him then groaned, clutching her skull between her hands. Even with her eyes scrunched closed in pain, she thought of him first. "Are you okay, Miguel?"

"I am now that you're awake," he tried to take his own advice and stay calm for her.

"How sweet." The man in charge gave a fake *awww*. Then he commanded his goon, "Get her up."

The guy grabbed for Sabine, latching on to her necklace. He snatched it in his meaty fist then yanked, choking her until the strands snapped.

"No!" Sabine fought like the wildcat she was then, landing a bunch of slaps and scratches before the guard subdued her, flinging her to the floor with a sickening *thud*.

"That's enough!" the well-dressed man shouted.

"Who are you? Why are you doing this?" Sabine asked as she got to her feet.

"Don't worry about that." He smiled. "Just worry about making your life something other than a living hell. You can do that by telling me where exactly you found the blue algae."

"Fuck you." Sabine spit at him.

Miguel winced even before the guard now inside her cell backhanded her. He rattled his cage door, bruising his fists as he pounded on the steel.

"Let's try this another way." The man jerked his chin toward Miguel and the second brute unlocked his door. Though he tried to rush the man, it didn't matter. There was nowhere for him to go and the guy was prepared. Soon they were both inside.

Miguel lunged at him. Still sluggish from whatever had given him the giant knot on the back of his head, he couldn't grab the guy before he landed a few solid punches that might have permanently changed the shape of Miguel's jaw.

Worse, the dude shook his fist then shoved it beneath his jacket and drew a gun. He pointed the thing straight between Miguel's eyes. Livid or not, he wasn't stupid. He stopped fighting and raised his hands, palms facing out in the universal sign for surrender.

"Would you like to reconsider your answer?" the slick guy asked Sabine.

"What are you going to do if I tell you?" she asked. "Steal it?"

"I guess you could say that." He didn't really answer her.

Miguel narrowed his eyes. What was this guy's angle?

"Don't tell them where it is, Sabine." He crossed his arms. "One life isn't worth it. Not mine."

The lackey in her cage pulled a matching gun to the one held by the guy in his cell and then they were equally threatened.

"Yours might not be." The guy in charge smirked. "But how about hers then?"

"Sabine, no!" Miguel didn't give a fuck about his own personal safety. If he witnessed her death, they might as well shoot him, too.

"Tell me where to find it," the man swiveled toward Sabine and repeated himself. "I have your laptop and your notes from the lab. I'm sure I can find the answer eventually. Help me get there faster, and I'll let your boyfriend go."

"Don't believe him!" Miguel knew how that would end.

The guy aiming his gun between Miguel's eyes didn't take kindly to that. He whacked Miguel in the temple with his gun, making him see stars again as his brain rattled around in his already bruised head.

"I can't watch you die over this, Miguel. Not you, too." Sabine fisted her hands. "He's got everything already. I don't care about glory. Let him publish my work and patent a cancer-fighting drug then sell it for premium prices only the ultra-elite can afford."

She winced at her own worst-case scenario before continuing, "Patents only last so long. It'll be available to the masses within a decade. And you'll be alive to see it."

"Don't," he warned her, until the man in her cage took a step closer and put the barrel of his gun directly against Sabine's head.

"That's really how you want today to end? With her impressive brains splattered across the wall?" the slick man asked. "That can be arranged. But it isn't necessary."

Miguel withered. Despite his instincts, he couldn't take the chance. "Forgive me, Sabine."

She stared, frozen, when he said, "The algae is at the base of Edge of the World. Seven-hundred and twenty-four feet underwater." Then he rattled off the coordinates he knew he'd never forget.

"We're in range still," the goon announced.

"Fire the missiles. Bombard the entire area. Then send the unmanned sub to confirm with photos. I want every last trace of it destroyed," the boss snarled. "If we fuck up this time, it'll be us that ends up swimming with the fishes."

"What?" Sabine looked back and forth between them as if trying to decide if this was some cosmic joke. "You're going to do *what*?"

"Your idea wasn't a bad one." The guy grinned. "However, my plans are much simpler than that. We're here to eliminate the algae and keep you from publishing anything about its existence."

"No!" Sabine shrieked. "Why? Why would you do that?"

"Because the clients I represent have fortunes invested in cancer treatment. Hospitals, equipment, expert doctors, and chemotherapy drugs that do a perfectly fine job of making buckets of money. If there's a cure...all that goes out the window." He frowned. "You're not going to eradicate the source of their income. Ruin their lives. They won't let that happen. You should have learned *that* from your mentor."

"That's ridiculous! What about all the lives it will save?"

She should have saved her breath, Miguel thought. Someone, or *someones*, as evil as this, who were driven by greed and selfishness, would never listen to reason. All the lives in the universe weren't nearly as important as their own financial security.

It didn't matter to them what the body count was so long as they could enjoy their spoils. He'd worked for clients like them sometimes as a divemaster.

Disgusting.

Sabine broke then. She pleaded. Told them she'd help them design other drugs to replace their cash flow. Promised to work for free in exchange for their reconsideration.

Instead, a rumble shook the entire boat.

Everyone froze, in shock or anticipation.

Then one of the goons grinned and relayed the message he'd received through his headset. "It's gone."

Time slowed to a crawl. A million things happened at once.

Sabine screamed. She launched herself at the man in her cage.

At the same time, the guy in Miguel's cell smirked. His trigger finger twitched.

Miguel braced himself.

A gunshot followed.

But not the one that would end his life. The man threatening him, however, wasn't so lucky.

He fell, dead before he hit the floor.

Soldiers, US Navy SEALs, stormed the brig. They captured the boss and as many of his accomplices as they could. Others, they killed. It was over in a matter of seconds.

Miguel rushed across the gap between their cells to Sabine. He cradled her in his arms, trying to quiet her hysterical wails. When he couldn't, he lifted her into his arms and headed for the exit, ignoring the shouts of the soldiers around them, but not before pausing to pluck her ruined necklace from the floor and tucking it into his pocket.

NINETEEN

Back on the *Divemaster*, Sabine sat in a stupor as they were debriefed by a combination of military personnel and her friends. Miguel hadn't left her side for an instant and Tosin had taken a seat on her other side, bracketing her.

"As a decorated pilot, Waverly had some pull when it came to the Navy. Captain Alex had even more. Together they reached out to high-ranking sources and explained the nature of the situation. Though Sabine and Miguel's lives were personally important to us, the recovery of the cancer cure prototype was certainly deserving of government intervention, so we focused on that in our plea for help," Archer explained.

"I appreciate everything you did," she mumbled.

"I wish they'd gotten there ten minutes sooner." He sighed, scrubbing his temples.

Just then the door opened and one of the WHOI staff who was still onboard entered the room. "I'm sorry to confirm that the algae bed is gone. Utterly destroyed. There's nothing left in a quarter mile radius of the site."

Sabine couldn't sit still a moment longer. She rocketed to her feet, frantic to search for any hint of the algae still alive.

"Where are you going, *lindeza*?" Miguel asked. He sounded surprised that even now she couldn't find it in her to quit.

"The lab. Or what's left of it. Maybe there's some residue on my equipment." Refusing to accept the truth, she ran to the dive platform and ducked under the crime scene tape keeping guests out of the fire-damaged area.

She had only one goal—to salvage some scrap of the prototype cure she'd whipped up yesterday and hope she could synthesize it in the lab. Make some artificial version with the same properties. Something. Anything. Even if it wasn't as potent as the original, natural substance, it could still be revolutionary in the fight against cancer.

Sabine stumbled when she saw the extent of the damage. Half-delirious, she staggered toward the ruins of her laboratory.

"Wait!" Miguel called after her. But she didn't.

She pawed through the debris, looking for a test tube, a Petri dish, *anything* that might have even a dot of algae on it. After a few minutes, and several new cuts, fresh blood was all she had to show for her efforts. Just like Heinrich's lab in Germany, her workspace had been leveled.

Now she knew why.

Sabine cursed. Not again. It couldn't all be for nothing.

"Hey, shhh." Miguel refused to back down this time. He bundled her in his arms and physically removed her from the wreckage. "The ocean is a huge place. We will find more. There could be other spots just like it along the channel somewhere. We didn't even look at a fraction of the seabed there."

In her heart, Sabine knew they could look forever. It wouldn't matter because it wasn't there to find. On the verge of losing her mind, she didn't see Banks approaching at first. He called softly to her, getting her attention when he waved her and Miguel over discreetly.

"Come with me, please. I need to show you something." He didn't wait for a response, striding from the room before any of the law enforcement officials could bog him down with requests or start asking too many questions.

They followed him to his office on the bridge of the ship in silence.

Captain Alex stood outside the door, feet spread, arms crossed, and a gun strapped openly to a holster around his waist.

Sabine looked at Miguel. He shrugged, unable to answer the questions assaulting her, but his spine straightened and he tugged her closer. If the captain felt there could still be danger, she trusted the guy. So did Miguel, apparently.

Neither of them could survive another threat like the one they'd lived through. She would never forget the moment she thought she would lose him, and how narrowly they had escaped even more tragedy today.

Banks turned to them and spoke in a whisper that had them huddling close. "When I set up the laboratory, I used the best practice standards of the American Chemical Society, which recommends daily backups."

"You've got copies of my files?" Sabine showed some interest at that, a tiny spark of her former self. "That's great, Banks. But that's not the most important thing. The algae. Without it...all I have is documentation for something that once existed and is now extinct."

She thought she might get sick admitting it.

"The protocols included duplication of files, notes, and office materials. It also specified proper storage of samples in redundant refrigeration units on separate power supplies in case of outages that could spoil entire research projects."

He changed their lives, and the world, with that one admission.

"You're saying you have a tiny bit of the algae preserved?" Sabine looked like a sea otter popping its head out of the water and glancing around, perking right up. "It's scary to work with such a limited resource, running tests and trying to figure out how to culture something we could accidentally annihilate in the process, but if we're careful... Please, tell me you did that."

"I did." He swallowed hard. "But it didn't turn out quite like I thought."

Fuck, how many ups and downs could they go through before they finally gave up? Sabine didn't know if she could handle another blow.

"You're scaring her, Banks." Captain Alex shook his head. "Get to the point."

Banks pointed to the edge of his door. That's when she noticed the faint blue light pulsing around it. "Is that—?"

Sabine rushed forward and flung open the door.

Algae covered every surface in a dripping blue goop.

"Apparently it doesn't mind being out of the water." Captain Alex chuckled. "It busted right through that wine chiller he hides his personal stash in and took over the place."

Globs plopped from the ceiling onto piles forming on the already coated floor.

"If this wasn't the most beautiful thing I have ever seen," Sabine whispered as if in a sacred temple, "it would be totally gross."

Captain Alex and Banks laughed.

Sabine whooped then launched herself at Banks. She kissed him with a giant, noisy smack, full on the lips. "We owe you everything. The *world* owes you."

"Hey, I guarded the door." Captain Alex tapped his toe, as if he could possibly be upset.

Sabine grinned, then treated their captain to the same effusive treatment before flying into Miguel's open arms for a decidedly steamier kiss.

Then, with one lingering glance at their miracle, they closed the door tight.

∿ TWENTY ∾

Miguel didn't bother talking to Sabine as they headed to his cabin. There wasn't much to say, nothing to compete with how he felt right then. He lifted her hand to his lips and kissed it a dozen times, though. When they closed the door behind them, safe inside their refuge, she whispered, "In the morning, I have to go. Waverly is coming for me as soon as the private jet is ready to take off."

He nodded once. "I know. However long it takes, I'll be here when you're ready to come back."

Nothing had changed since she'd argued that this was his place.

In his heart, he believed she'd been right. Except that without her, it wouldn't be the same.

From his pocket, he withdrew the broken necklace she'd worn during her stay. He grabbed the small tool kit he used for working on his gear from one of his shelves then plopped into the desk chair to repair it as best he could. In order to reattach the part that had been torn, directly in the center, he used some monofilament he had in his tackle box then drilled a small hole in an unusual shell he'd pocketed on one of their collection dives.

When he'd finished, the shell looked like it had always been there. It dangled from the line that now hung down off the main strand of the necklace and would land somewhere at the top of her cleavage.

He stood, surprised to find her nude, sitting on the edge of the bed behind him, watching.

Miguel smiled as he approached, holding out his gift. She pulled her hair off to the side then lifted her chin, giving him full access to her graceful neck.

"This belongs to you." He fastened the homemade jewelry, hoping it might remind her of him during the long months ahead. "Same as I do."

"I wish I had something to give you in return." She frowned until he kissed the downward curve of her lips.

"All I want is you." He stripped off the shirt and shorts he'd donned in a matter of moments when the fire alarms had roused him earlier. Naked, he leaned down and into her, taking her to her back on their bed.

"You already have that, Miguel." She kissed him tenderly then paused, staring up at him as she promised, "I love you."

His heart seemed to do a backward roll right there in his chest.

"Thank you." She hadn't had to give him that reassurance. In some ways it made things messier, but he was so glad she had. "I love you too, *lindeza*."

He covered her completely then, hoping to impress himself on every inch of her. He entwined their fingers and brought her hands up beside her head before kissing her endlessly. Or for as long as he dared, knowing their time could run out any moment now.

His body moved over hers, reveling in the caress of her skin over his, even as he tried to imprint himself on her. Without taking his hands from her, he glided across her until his cock aligned with her opening.

It took longer than if he'd let go of her to guide himself inside, but he didn't want to do that until he had to. So he used his hips to work himself into her bit by bit. It seemed only fair since she'd done something similar to him, taking up residence in his heart during her time onboard.

Sabine gasped, her mouth opening as she concentrated on the pleasure he imparted.

He took advantage, kissing her, rubbing his lips over hers softly before licking along just the tip of her tongue. The barest of contacts set them both on fire.

Though he tried to drag out their lovemaking for hours, the sense of urgency built fairly quickly. Desperation began to seep from him and it manifested in the driving thrusts of his cock through her clenching rings of muscle.

Sabine's legs shifted, hugging him tight as she prepared to shatter.

And when they came, they came together.

Her pussy milked every drop of come from his balls, holding as much of him as he could give deep within her. Completely empty, he crashed to the mattress and drew her on top of his heaving chest. He wrapped his arms around her and didn't let her go.

Until he had to.

A while later, a knock on the door startled them both. Miguel called out, "Yes?"

"It's time," Waverly answered, reminding him of a guard calling a prisoner to execution. He had to keep reminding himself that this was the opportunity of a lifetime for her and one that would end suffering for millions of people.

A broken heart meant nothing compared to that.

Two broken hearts even.

He kissed Sabine one last time, until the sheen in her pretty eyes receded some. "Ready?"

"No." She stood and dressed then grabbed her purse, not bothering to pack her suitcase. Having her things there would be a comfort to him even if it was an illusion. "But I'm going anyway."

Miguel nodded. "You've got this."

They marched to the helicopter together, as if they were walking the plank.

He was surprised to see not one, but three other choppers circling the *Divemaster* when they got there.

"Uncle Sam is committed to providing security for the trip and in the undisclosed location where they're setting up Sabine's temporary laboratory. She's going to be fine, Miguel," Waverly promised.

He nodded, but it didn't feel *fine*.

Not when her palm was sweaty against his, though her fingers felt like ice.

Brave and glorious, she stood beneath the wash of the propellers, her hair rioting around her. His sea glass and shell necklace made her look like some ocean goddess.

Miguel couldn't possibly have loved her more. He told her so in between kisses, taking one more and one more until there were no one mores left.

Tosin, Archer, Banks, and Captain Alex stood at the edge of the helipad, waving as Sabine climbed into the helicopter. She turned just before shutting the door and said, "I love you, Miguel."

"I love you, too. Until next time..." He lifted his hand to wave. It had been impossible to say goodbye.

"As soon as I can, even if that's years." She winced then blew him and the rest of their little gang kisses before disappearing inside.

He stood on the deck and watched the flock of helicopters as they raced for the shores of Maui and the private jet that would at least ensure her comfort until she got wherever they were taking her.

And then she was gone.

✺ TWENTY-ONE ✺

Miguel sat at the long outdoor dining table, pushing food around his plate without any intention of eating the rest of it. Nothing seemed appetizing. Hell, even diving didn't sound very good right now. Maybe Tosin wouldn't mind guiding Miguel's group today.

It took a while, but he finally realized that his friends had stopped talking. They exchanged worried glances over his head. He pretended not to notice. After all, what could he say? That he was fine?

Everyone onboard knew that was a lie.

Tosin broke their silence. "Dude, when are you going to quit moping and go after Sabine?"

"You want me to leave?" It pissed him off after what he'd given up to stay.

"Of course we don't," Banks jumped in then. "But it's clear that being here without her isn't good for you anymore."

Archer and Waverly held hands as they studied him. He hated the pity in their stares. Waverly tried to smooth things over. "I know how you feel. It was hell being apart from Archer. I did it for ten years. Don't recommend it, either. To be perfectly honest, the first few were miserable and the ache never entirely went away. I regret how much time we wasted. None of us want that for you."

"We'll be here when you're ready to come home. *With* Sabine," Archer promised.

"Won't you need another partner? Someone to fill my spot?" He cleared his throat then spoke one of his worst fears aloud. "It could take *years*. Will I have to sell my share in the *Divemaster* so you can keep going without me?"

Now he was glad he hadn't eaten much—otherwise he'd probably be hanging over the railing like a landlubber who hadn't gotten his sea legs yet. Still, they were right. If that's what it took, he'd do it.

Living without Sabine wasn't living at all.

She'd been gone for a month and though they tried to talk every day, the truth was that she was busy with incredibly important things. Given her schedule and the crazy time differences between them, it was tough. He felt like he was losing touch with her.

It'd been three days since she'd even answered his emails.

Maybe she hadn't had nearly as much trouble forgetting about him as he'd had moving on without her. *Shit.*

"Don't be a dumbass." Tosin shoved him. "No one is letting you cash out. You'll come back. Eventually."

Why didn't that do much to make Miguel feel better? Probably because his friend didn't seem hundred-percent confident even as he said it.

He nodded, then tossed his balled up napkin onto his plate. "Okay."

It was time to find his woman, wherever she might be in the world right now.

That turned out to be a far easier task than he'd imagined. When he stood, he noticed a sleek powerboat racing directly toward the *Divemaster*, which was now anchored off the coast of Kauai.

Banks pulled out his cell phone and had someone—probably Captain Alex—on the other line instantly. "Are we expecting visitors?"

They'd gotten jumpy after first Waverly's trouble and then the attack on Sabine. Having people board the *Divemaster* had been an enormous violation, one none of them would forget anytime soon.

"Ah, thank you." Banks was grinning now.

"Who is it?" Archer asked.

But Miguel didn't need to hear the answer. A woman waved from the boat, golden curls flying everywhere. Sabine! She'd come back to him.

He charged across the deck and down the stairs to the landing area, sprinting by the time he made it to the gangway.

Sabine seemed equally ready to be back in his arms. She didn't bother to wait until the boat had finished docking before flying over the edge at him. He smothered her in a bear hug as he carried her onto the boat and deposited her in the midst of their friends.

After stealing several kisses, he said, "I guess I see why you haven't been responding to my messages."

"Sorry, I wanted to surprise you. But there were delays and my luggage got lost and...ugh, you know how it goes when traveling halfway around the world.”

“Why wouldn’t you have called for the private jet?” Banks asked.

She blinked a few times. “I guess I’m still not quite used to the way you all roll.”

“Well, you’d better get used to it.” Miguel crushed her to him. “Because I’m not letting go of you again. How long can you stay? I’m going with you when you have to leave.”

“What if I want to stay forever?” she asked, making his heart start to pound in his chest.

“Can you do that?” he wondered. “Without jeopardizing the drug development or giving up on your career, I mean? Of course you’re welcome for as long as you like.”

She kissed him again, as if she needed to reassure herself they were truly together again.

He knew the feeling.

“Maybe?” She shrugged. “It’ll take some creativity to make it work, and some traveling, but I was miserable without you, Miguel.”

Sabine blushed, as if uncomfortable with admitting it.

“You couldn’t have been any more pathetic than this guy.” Tosin slapped Miguel on the back.

“I don’t know about that.” She toyed with his necklace. “Even if I have to make some serious sacrifices, this is where I want to be.”

Miguel wrapped her up in his arms again, afraid he might be dreaming about this as he had so many times in the past several weeks.

Banks waited until they had settled down a little before asking, “Where do you stand with everything? If you let me know where you are and what needs to be done still, I'm more than happy to help you in any way. I'm sure if we work together, we can arrange anything you need."

Sabine smiled and crossed to Banks, hugging him as well. "I missed you, too, Banks."

He ruffled her hair as if she were a little girl.

"Well, I'm happy to say they put our patent through on a rush due to the unusual circumstances and whatever you did to motivate them. Once I had it in hand, the very first thing I did was publicly post every scrap of research I had. I plastered every open source science database on the Internet with pictures, descriptions, chemical compounds, trial results. Everything. I figured that's where both Heinrich and I went wrong. Trying to keep it under wraps was pointless. This way, no one can try to steal it or say it doesn't exist or whatever." She winced. "The drug companies that had been fighting over me and the right to produce any future drug that comes of my work are pretty pissed about it, but I don't give a fuck. I'm not taking the chance of anything being lost. That information belongs to the world, not people looking to make a buck. Besides, if it's all out there, there's no reason for people to hunt me anymore, right? They know everything I know. Or at least that's how I figured it."

Archer held out his fist for her to bump. Of course he would approve. It wasn't so dissimilar to what he was trying to do with his inheritance. In fact...

His best friend made the suggestion Miguel had just nearly proposed.

"Look, no pressure or anything, but why not work for the Banks Foundation? We'll pay you ten times whatever the next competitive offer is." Archer waved away her protests. "My only stipulation would be that someday, when the drug is ready, you let us give it away. I want this cure to be available to everyone, everywhere."

Sabine sagged, as if she'd been too afraid to hope for such a blessing. "That's what I was hoping for. It's what Heinrich would have wanted, too, though he might not have had the choice. To fund his research, he would have had to sell rights to a private firm."

"Or maybe the Banks Foundation would have found him—and you—anyway." Banks shrugged. "Life is kind of funny like that sometimes."

Miguel couldn't keep his hands off Sabine. Not because he wanted to fuck her so bad his dick might fall off soon—though he did—but because he couldn't believe everything could go from shit to sugar so fast.

"So I'll start making some arrangements." Banks never seemed to grow tired of providing for them. It truly seemed to make him happy to give them whatever they needed. "I'll start with refitting a section of the lower deck for a proper laboratory. Give me a list later of what improvements you'll require."

"Honestly..." Sabine smiled then. "The algae is remarkably easy to work with. Kind of like the penicillin of the sea. I thought it over on my flights here and I can't imagine anything we couldn't easily get for the ship. Some space, some time, some funding...I've got this."

"What about human trials?" Archer asked. "I realize that could be a while yet, but if we enhance our medical bay, could we do them at sea? Expand the Divemaster Project. I mean, who's more deserving of a vacation than people willing to put their lives on the line for the advancement of science, while hopefully finding a cure for themselves?"

"Wow." She blinked. "I hadn't thought of that yet, but…yes, I don't see why not."

Miguel couldn't believe how amazing she was. He was willing to support her however necessary to guarantee her success. Both for her, and for everyone who would benefit from her work. "And when you need to travel, I'll go with you."

"I would love that." She bit her lip. "There's something else I kind of had you in mind for…"

Tosin cracked up. "Oh, can I guess? Can I guess?"

"Not that." Sabine blushed. "Well, okay, yes…that. But something else."

"How can I help?" he asked.

"As long as I live, I'll never get the feeling of them obliterating that algae bed from my mind." She shuddered.

Miguel drew her close to him and held her tight. "Me either."

"So I think we should start algae farms. Wherever we happen to travel to. It's easy to grow, as Banks found out for us, but I think we should do some research into how to manage it responsibly, without introducing a foreign species to the natural environments. Somehow, though, we need to create contained grow houses or something to give as much redundancy as possible to the supply."

"I'd love to take that on." He started dreaming up systems they could build and implement. Underwater harvest stations that he could service on deep-water technical dives that would challenge him over and over. "Sign me up."

"Perfect! So…about those trips I might have to take on occasion…" Sabine lit up.

"Yeah, you have one planned already?" he asked.

"Nothing concrete." She shook her head as if in disbelief. "But I've been told that if this pans out, I should expect to attend the award ceremonies for the Nobel Prize in Chemistry in a year or two with a speech, prepared to accept since they don't allow posthumous nominations. They said I could talk about Heinrich as much as I wanted, though."

"Whoa." Even Tosin didn't have a smart ass remark for that.

"Yeah." She held her hands out, palms up. "I hope no one will mind if I name the drug after him."

"That's a lovely idea." Banks squeezed her shoulder. "I'm sure Marta will appreciate the gesture. Maybe she'll come check out our operations sometime. And she certainly wouldn't miss such an important day in your life. If it comes to pass, and I have faith it will, I'd volunteer to be her date to the ceremony."

"Subtle, Banks. Reaaal subtle," Tosin teased.

They all laughed. Sabine included. "Hey, leave him alone. I sincerely hope everyone I love finds as much happiness as I have with Miguel. Banks and Tosin, you especially."

"Are you thinking what I'm thinking," Waverly asked Sabine.

"Definitely." They grinned at Tosin. "We should team up to do some matchmaking for our final single divemaster."

"Oh no. *No.*" He waved them off. "I'm perfectly fine living this bachelor life over here. Don't start slinging your relationship cooties on me."

"You don't know what you're missing," Archer promised.

"But when you realize it, we'll gladly say I told you." Miguel punched Tosin's biceps then spun to Sabine. He'd had enough talking for one afternoon.

Now it was time to welcome her home the right way.

He threw her over his shoulder as he had the first time he'd taken her to the clubroom, then marched below deck to make some more memories. The first of many in their new life together.

ABOUT THE AUTHOR

Jayne Rylon is a *New York Times* and *USA Today* bestselling author. She received the 2011 RomanticTimes Reviewers' Choice Award for Best Indie Erotic Romance.

Her stories used to begin as daydreams in seemingly endless business meetings, but now she is a full-time author, who employs the skills she learned from her straight-laced corporate existence in the business of writing. She lives in Ohio with two cats and her husband, the infamous Mr. Rylon.

When she can escape her purple office, Jayne loves to travel the world, SCUBA dive, take pictures, avoid speeding tickets in her beloved Sky and—of course—read.

www.ingramcontent.com/pod-product-compliance
Lightning Source LLC
Chambersburg PA
CBHW071303190726
48292CB00007B/2667